# EVIL

# IN THE

# WOODS

## A TWISTED TIMBERS THRILLER

Kevin M. Moehring

*"Rock bottom became the solid foundation on which I rebuilt my life."*

-- J. K. Rowling

*For those of you who stood by me when I was not a good person, always knowing I was capable of much more. It did not go unnoticed.*

This is a work of fiction. Names, characters, places, and incidents are all the product of the author's imagination or are used fictitiously, and any resemblance to actual persons, living or dead, business establishments, events, or locales is entirely coincidental. The publisher does not have any control over and does not assume any responsibility for author or third-party websites or their content.

ISBN: 978-1-7321567-0-8

# *Chapter 1*

The gavel comes down firm and the sentencing is complete, thus ending a tumultuous time in the life of Mitch Thompson. The jurors are escorted out of their seats and into the hidden room behind the judge's chambers. The bailiffs lead the convicted murderer through a different door, and straight to the prison where he will serve out his life sentence. Lawyers are shuffling through the papers on their desks, shoving file folders into their briefcases. Finally, the spectators begin to rise and make their way out into the hallway. One by one they begin talking about the case and making statements regarding the facts.

Mitch Thompson is one of the last to leave the court room. He remains in his seat, rubbing his sweaty palms along his pleated khakis to dry the sweat that has formed on his palms. He doesn't speak to anyone as he makes his way through the groups of people who have formed outside the courtroom. He untucks his button-down shirt as he makes his way down the spiral staircase and out the main door of the building, he walks quickly and heads straight for his truck. Reporters have gathered and are fighting for the chance to get a quote from the one spectator who was part of the case itself. He puts his head down and fights his way through the crowd, managing to cross the street and get away from the microphones without uttering a word.

He has become used to this routine. He made a vow to the convicted prisoner that he would be present at every court appearance until the man got what was coming to him. Now in the safety of his truck, Mitch can relax for the first time all day. It is not often you watch a former colleague and friend get sentenced to life in prison for the murder of your father. Today marks the end of a long three months for Mitch, since the events at Graham Park changed his life forever. His days have been filled with countless trips to Portland for the trial, trying to rebuild the police force of Twisted Timbers and handling the duties that come from the influx of visitors to the area. The national media attention has caused a normally busy tourist season to be much larger than other years. Every news station in the country has flocked to the small town and taken full advantage of the picturesque views the town boasts to help sell their story.

As he turns his truck off the interstate and onto Highway 30, heading west towards his small town, Sheriff Mitch Thompson is lost in his thoughts. The green lush forests and the bright sunshine has a way of making a person lose concentration and get lost in their imagination. The road winds back and forth, following the terrain along the way. Patches of pavement are covered in bright sunlight that has won the fight and made its way through the trees. Other portions are as dark as night, the overhanging trees working hard to prevent the rays from the sun from breaking through and reach the ground below.

Mitch has traveled this road so many times over the last three months that he hardly pays attention as he takes the long, sweeping turns several miles an hour above the posted speed limit. He is almost to the turn onto Main Street before he remembers that he hadn't checked his phone since he went into the court house. He pulls the phone out of his jacket pocket and flips it open. The screen lights up and tells him he has five missed calls and three voice messages. He checks the numbers for the missed calls and sees that four of them are from Lucille Pennington, the receptionist at the police station. The final missed call came from the cell phone of Stuart Johnson, the longest tenured member of the police force and the only other person to make it out of Graham Park successfully.

Since he is only five minutes from the station and the fact that there is rarely any cell service on Highway 30, Mitch decides to just drive to the station without calling in. He has gotten several messages during his trips to Portland in the past, rarely does it lead to anything important. Since the hiring of the two new officers, his duties have been extremely lightened. He is still the town sheriff, so he is called upon to make the tough decisions and handle the unusual cases, something he never wanted to be responsible for.

The streets of town are busy for a Thursday afternoon. To say that the town was prepared for the increase in popularity and the extra hordes of people that come to town for the weekends would be a lie. They've had to add a temporary stoplight in the center of town, a nuisance that Mitch is hating at the moment as he sits at the stagnant red light. Before he can even mumble out a swear word, the light changes to green and Mitch drives the last block, pulling into his reserved spot in front of the station.

The halls of the station are quiet. With the number of missed calls he received, Mitch expected there to be chaos inside the walls of the building. Lucille is the only other person in the office, sitting quietly at her desk and tapping away on a computer. "Hey Lucille, where is everyone? I had a bunch of missed calls, I thought the town would be gone when I got back."

Lucille practically jumps out of her seat at the sound of his voice. "Sheriff, you startled me. I didn't hear you come in." She looks up at the young sheriff with a welcoming smile. "How did things go in Portland? Did you get the outcome you wanted?"

"I guess you can say he got what he deserved. I'm not sure what I was expecting but I'm glad the system worked." He was honest in his assessment. It's hard for a man to know how he is supposed to feel after watching his former friend sentenced to life in prison, even if he did kill his father. "What were all of the calls to my cell phone about?"

Lucille once again looks as if she is taken off-guard by the question. "Oh that, it's probably nothing, but you know how Stuart is. We got a few calls from hikers who claim they saw a man running around in the woods with an axe. The callers couldn't describe the man very much. They said he was dressed in all black and moved very quickly. In fact, one caller claimed that it wasn't even a man." She stops long enough to thumb through a stack of papers before pulling one out and looking it over. "Here it is, the person started the call by asking if there had been any reports of Bigfoot in the area. So, like I said, I wouldn't worry about it too much. You know how these city folks can be when they get in touch with nature."

"I guess so," Mitch takes the caller form from Lucille and looks it over for his own recollection. "I'm guessing Stuart went to check it out?"

"Yeah, he took Deputy Carter with him. They were heading out to Hidden Creek to look around. Like I said, it's probably nothing." She turns her head away and begins studiously typing away, probably filling out the forms that record every phone call that comes into the station.

"Let's hope so. I'm not sure this town can take any more excitement. The weekends have already gotten to be almost more than we can handle." Mitch opens the door to his private office and turns to speak to Lucille once more. "You should take advantage of things while it's quiet, get out of here and get some rest while you can. I'm going to work on some paperwork and wait to hear from Johnson and Carter. Nichols should be here shortly to start the night shift. I want to make sure she knows what to expect this weekend."

"I'm just about done here, trying to get the hang of this new computer is driving me insane. You know, I really like that Deputy Nichols. Now Carter, you can send him back to Portland for all I care. It's nice to have another woman in the office." Lucille has never been afraid to share her opinions on how things should be run at the station. "Plus, I see the way you look at her."

Mitch blushes at the last statement. He can't say that the receptionist isn't telling the truth, he had just hoped that no one had noticed. Deputy Nichols is definitely an attractive woman, but she is also an employee. Mitch knows better than to mix business with pleasure. He closes the door and sits down at his desk, the same desk that was once used by his father.

# *Chapter 2*

Sitting alone in his quiet office is not exactly what Mitch was hoping to do tonight. In the three months since his father passed away, he has tried to stay busy. Breaking in two new officers and the dozens of trips into Portland has helped keep his mind off the fact that he lost the only family he had left. On the slow nights around town, Mitch would usually find himself sitting at the bar at the Bottom Dollar, the very spot where he arrested his father's killer. Growing up, even when his friends were having late night parties, Mitch was never much of a drinker. Now that he puts in twelve to fourteen-hour days on a regular basis, a beer at the end of the shift has become routine.

The ringing of the phone on his desk snaps him out of his haze. He picks it up and sounds rather upset when he answers. "Twisted Timbers Police Department, Sheriff Thompson speaking."

"Hey Sheriff, I didn't expect you to pick up. It's Stuart and I've been out here in the woods by Hidden Creek having a look around. I'm not sure what those people saw but I'm not finding anybody out here swinging an axe around." The older man sounds like he is out of breath; trying to keep up with the much younger and much more physically fit Deputy Carter is almost impossible.

"I didn't expect you would find anything. It was probably just some folks from the big city who aren't used to the shadows and sounds that come along with being so deep in the woods. Head on back to the station and fill in Deputy Nichols when you get here. I'm going to head home once she shows up." Mitch knows that he will not be heading home but he doesn't want it to be common knowledge that he has become a regular at the bar.

"Will do Sheriff. Hey, I heard about the sentence. I guess we can finally put all of that Graham Park nonsense behind us." Stuart has not been the same since the events of that night. Neither has Sheriff Thompson.

"I guess you can say that. We just move on day by day and get on with our lives. Make sure you file a report about tonight, I'll need to look it over in the morning." Mitch hangs up the phone without waiting for a response from Stuart. He looks up from his computer long enough to watch Sloane Nichols walk in through the front door and head for the locker room where the deputies get dressed.

Deputy Nichols is the most recent addition to the police department. Mitch has no idea when she showed up or why she came to town. One day he found her resume on his desk, complete with a list of recommendations from the L.A.P.D. He was taken aback by her appearance the first time they met. He wasn't sure what he was expecting when she walked into his office, but Mitch still has an old-fashioned idealism. The fact that a woman that looks as good as she does would want to be a police officer is not something that had ever crossed his mind.

She is a few years older than Mitch, in her mid-twenties, but the two of them are by far the youngest officers on the force. They have more in common with each other than they do with any of their co-workers. They tend to have conversations regarding popular music or television shows, things that the older generation just wouldn't understand. He has managed to keep his relationship with her strictly professional up until now. The fact is, he knows very little about her personal life, or why she came to Twisted Timbers in the first place. As she exits the locker room and heads for his office door, he fumbles with some papers to make it appear he is fast at work and he hadn't been watching her walk through the hall.

"Sheriff Thompson, I didn't expect to see you here tonight." She gives him the bright smile that he's certain made her popular with the boys in high school.

"I'm just finishing up some things before heading out. Listen, there were some calls that came in today. Apparently, some hikers claim they saw a man wielding an axe and running through the woods. Johnson and Carter were out by Hidden Creek all day checking it out. They're headed back now and will fill you in when they get here." He shoves some files from on top of his desk into a drawer, once again trying to look busy.

"Oh, maybe some action for a change. I could go for a little excitement in my life." Sloane giggles a little and lets out a half-smile that lets the sheriff know that she is only mildly serious.

"Yeah, I wouldn't bet on it. Just be on your toes and make sure you document every call that comes in. I'll want to look over the reports in the morning." He lets his last words trail off as he makes his way to his feet and throws on his hat.

"Just like a man. Get my hopes up with thoughts of excitement and actual police work. Then you leave me here all by my lonesome." It's just in her nature to make everything she says sound like an attempt to flirt. She doesn't do it on purpose, at least she tells herself that every chance she gets.

"Sorry to let you down, but this is a small town where nothing ever happens. If you came here because of what you saw on the news, I'm sorry to tell you that nothing like that will probably ever happen again." Every fiber in his being is hoping that he will never have to deal with anything that serious again. "Now if you'll excuse me, it's been a long day."

"Sure thing Sheriff. By the way, when you get there, make sure you have a drink for me. Lord knows I could use one or two."

# Kevin M. Moehring

# *Chapter 3*

The short drive over to the Bottom Dollar is just long enough for Mitch to get lost in his thoughts about Deputy Nichols. Is he imagining the fact that everything she says to him comes across as a pick-up line, or is she honestly trying to hit on him. The fact that he has never had a steady girlfriend in his life has led him to live in solitude and naivete about how women act. He dismisses her advances as just friendly banter between co-workers as he pulls into the parking lot of the bar.

From the moment he enters the front door, Mitch regrets his decision to come here. He had forgotten the fact that it's a Thursday night, when drink prices are at the lowest to help bring in the visitors who arrive early for the weekend. On top of the cheap beers, it's also karaoke night. His ears are assaulted by three college-aged girls doing a great injustice to a classic Cyndi Lauper tune. The bar is small, very small, with only about four tables in the sitting area and a dozen or so stools lining the bar. Sheriff Thompson is relieved to see the last stool is vacant and he makes his way there.

The bartender must have seen him come in and has his beer in front of him before Mitch can even remove his hat. He nods to the female server and she walks away and begins mixing liquor drinks. Mitch scans the room and even though he is just about the youngest person in the room, he feels like he is the chaperone at a grade school party. Pitchers of beer are stacked on every table, most of them empty. Even though he comes to the bar more frequently than he would like to admit, he is confident in the fact that he has never let himself get as intoxicated as most of these folks are.

The looks he gets from the patrons whenever he walks in is an odd one. He has never experienced fame before. Most of the people look at him like they have seen him before, but they can't place where they know him from. Usually when they get a look at his badge, they either become quiet thinking he is on-duty, or they want to come over and talk to him. Luckily the college girls did a decent job of masquerading his entrance to the rest of the bar and he was able to avoid the uncomfortable stares.

With a long drink from the bottle he finishes his first beer and nods to the bartender to bring him another. He watches as she finishes making a few mixed drinks, reaches into the cooler and pops the metal top from his next bottle. She places it down in front of him and turns away without saying a word. She has seen him in here enough times to know that he is a low maintenance customer, unlike the tourists who expect five-star service. He drinks the same thing every time he comes in and rarely will he have more than three before paying his tab, tipping well and leaving for the night. No sooner had he began to sip on his new beer and he could feel the vibration from his cell phone in his pocket.

The bar is extremely loud, with so much horrible singing going on in such a tiny room. He races to the front door to try and drown out the last verse of a Neil Diamond song that he detests. "Hello, this is Sheriff Thompson."

"Sheriff, it's Nichols. I hate to bother you, but I have an old man here, he says he's the owner of the Hidden Creek Campground. Apparently, there was a younger couple staying in one of his cabins and they failed to check-out this afternoon."

Mitch is pacing around the front door of the bar. The music slips through the walls like a steady reminder of how much he hates karaoke and the people that sing it. "Maybe they decided to leave early this morning and the owner wasn't in the office to check them out."

"No Sheriff, Mr. Blevins here says that all their belongings were still in the cabin. He said the last time he saw them was yesterday afternoon. They were headed out for a hike along Hidden Creek." She is firm in her tone of voice, to show the sheriff that she's confident more is going on than what he initially thought.

"Alright. I'll head back over there and talk to Mr. Blevins myself. Let me go back inside and pay my tab." Part of him is happy to be put out of his misery, not sure how much more awful singing he could take. However, this is one aspect of being sheriff that he hates the most. No matter what he is doing in his personal life, he is expected to come running at the first sign of something serious.

"You probably have time to grab the microphone and belt out an old country tune. Sorry, I shouldn't have said that." Sloane is aware of how her comments can be taken as flirtatious, but she only apologizes when she says them at the wrong time. "Do you think this is somehow connected to the calls that came in earlier today? The ones about the man with the axe."

**Kevin M. Moehring**

# *Chapter 4*

Mitch walks quickly back through the bar and lays a twenty near his half full beer. He nods at the bartender and walks even faster out of the building. He fires up his truck with his mind more focused on the flirtatious female deputy than it is on the reason he needs to head back to the station. He has had a few girlfriends in his twenty-one years, none of them ever got past the innocent kissing stage. Since he started on the police force immediately after graduation, he never really had time to get serious with anyone. Now, he has no idea what to do regarding members of the opposite sex, and with his father no longer around, he has lost the person who would normally teach a young man about such things.

The moon is full over the Oregon night, coating the town in the warm glow of its light as Mitch steers his truck into his reserved spot. He throws in a piece of gum to mask the smell of the beer on his breath as he takes the steps two at a time and slings open the front door. The glass door hits the back wall much harder than he expected it to and the sound it makes reverberates through the long hall. He can see the back of Mr. Blevins as he enters the primary office. The man is short, and his gray hair is tucked under his familiar black hat. Mitch has seen him dozens of times over the years and has never seen the man without that hat on.

"Mr. Blevins, how are we tonight?" He makes his way to the opposite side of the desk and smiles at Deputy Nichols in the process.

"I'm good Sheriff, it's good to see you again. Before I forget, I never had a chance to give you my condolences about your father. He was a good man and this town will miss him." The man looks like he has aged severely over the last few years. The missing teeth are far more prevalent as he gives the new sheriff his sympathetic smile.

"Thanks Tom, I appreciate it. My deputy here tells me you have some concerns about a couple of hikers who didn't check out?" The office is the last place Mitch wants to be at this particular moment, but it does give him a second chance to see Deputy Nichols.

"They were supposed to check out this afternoon. A young couple in their early twenties who were in town from Seattle. I try not to pay too much attention to the people that stay at the campground, but it isn't usually very crowded during the week. Plus, I can't stand people from Seattle. They come down here with their long hair and those brightly colored football jerseys and they think they own the place. Anyway, I noticed them leaving with backpacks yesterday, sometime around noon."

"Let me stop you there. Is there a chance that they had a tent in those backpacks? I'm thinking maybe they left out on a hike to spend the night along the creek and then they got turned around and couldn't find their way out of the woods tonight." His father always had a way of looking at the obvious solutions to the problem, hoping that there is always a simple solution. Mitch spent much of his youth watching his old man diffuse situations in this manner and has learned a thing or two. "It's possible that they decided to set up camp for another night and they'll turn up in the morning."

"It's possible, but they looked to me like they were experienced hikers. They had plenty of equipment with them." The old man stops speaking and considers the possibility of what Mitch said once more. "I mean, I guess it could be possible. It wouldn't be the first time we had some city folks who got lost in the woods, would it?"

Mitch lets out a smile and looks at Deputy Nichols, herself being a transplant from Los Angeles. "It certainly would not. They call it Hidden Creek for a reason." The fact that it takes a twenty-minute hike to even find the creek usually scares away the beginner hikers.

"Yeah, I guess you're right. What do you suggest I do with their belongings? You know how busy the weekends have been this season and I can't really afford to lose the rental money." Once again, he stops before finishing his thought and it's clear to both men that worrying about money seems slightly inappropriate when they could be talking about two missing hikers. "I care about the well-being of the couple as well, but you know we depend on the revenue during the peak season to survive the winter."

"Tom, I know as good as anyone the importance of the tourist revenue. I suggest you gather up their things and store them in your cabin. If they aren't back by the afternoon, then give me a call and we can go from there. That way you will have ample time to get the site ready for your weekend renters." He looks at the old man waiting for a response. The silence in the room causes everyone to become uncomfortable.

"You know that means more work for me," says Tom. The thought of more work has made the old man slightly agitated. "I'm getting a little too old to be cleaning up after these yuppies, let alone packing up their personal effects."

"I understand what you're saying but maybe you can add a little fee to their total when they check out. You can call it service fee or a cleaning fee. Heck, you can call it whatever you want. You'll have their belongings and if they refuse to pay, you are within your rights to keep their things." Mitch knows that mentioning more money will get the man's attention and hopefully bring a satisfactory resolution to the issue.

The man looks at the sheriff with bigger eyes and turns his head toward Deputy Nichols. Mitch might be young, but he has been around long enough to know that the business owners in the small town will do just about anything if it means they will be able to make more money. He uses this to relieve the tension in the room and judging by the change in Mr. Blevins's facial expressions, it's working.

The man nods in agreement, extends his hand to shake Mitch's and turns to head out of the station. He seems satisfied as he leaves, never looking back to Mitch or Sloane. As soon as Mr. Blevins leaves the room, the two officers look at each other and there is an obvious tension between the two. Luckily, the awkwardness is broken when Deputy Johnson and Carter enter the room. They are finally returning from their trip to Hidden Creek and have the look of two men who have gotten a little too close to nature.

"Welcome back boys. Looks like you guys had fun playing in the woods today." Mitch is happy to see the other two deputies, so he is not forced to talk to Sloane more than is necessary. "Were you able to find any trace of the mystery man with the axe, or as one caller stated, did you find Bigfoot?"

"We found nothing, but I was able to give the new guy a good workout. These young people have no endurance." Stuart has always been the one in the office to be able to poke fun at his fellow officers. His comedic relief has been much needed and even more appreciated through the last few months.

"I needed more endurance, so I could pick you up every time you tripped over a branch." Deputy Jerome Carter has a deep voice and stands head and shoulders above the other men. "We could have been back a half an hour ago, if Stuart didn't get the truck stuck in the mud."

It's a rare occasion that all four officers are in the station at the same time. With the two new officers being thrown into service without much time for training on how things are normally done in Twisted Timbers, these moments of comradery are the best times for them to learn how each other works and get used to the array of personalities.

"Well you may have seen Mr. Blevins leaving as you came in. He claims there's a couple of hikers that failed to check out this afternoon and he thinks they are lost in the woods. I convinced him to gather their belongings, so he can rent the space tomorrow, and if the couple doesn't turn up, we may have to head out to the creek again. I'm thinking they may have lost track of time or gotten off the path and decided to camp for the night and will show up in the morning."

"Well if we need to hike back in there tomorrow, I need to get my old body home and in bed." Stuart is twice the age of Mitch and has never been on the athletic side. "Anyone want to stop at the diner for a bite to eat?"

"I thought you need to get to bed?" Carter is already taking off his black boots and looks like a man defeated. "I could go for a bite to eat though. Let me get out of this uniform and I'll go with you."

"You boys go ahead, I'm going to head on home. As long as Sloane has things under control, that is." He looks at the female deputy and she gives him the smile that shows off her white teeth.

"You guys go feed your faces. I am more than capable of handling this place alone. Besides, I'm tougher than any of you fools anyway." Nichols loves to make the men feel like she can do anything better than they can. Her competitive nature is one of the things that Mitch finds the most attractive about her.

Carter and Johnson both head to the locker room to change out of their uniforms. Mitch turns and heads to his office. He didn't really need anything from his office, but he also didn't want to be left alone with Sloane. He has an uneasy feeling whenever they are alone. Not like something bad is going to happen, but more of a feeling that he wants to get closer to her than is acceptable, especially since he is her boss. He sits down in his chair long enough to steal a look out the window and see her leaning against the main counter in the reception area. Her blonde hair is pulled up in a ponytail, forming a curl at the bottom. She waves to the other two male officers as they leave for the night and turns her head quickly and catches his eyes affixed on her backside.

Mitch reacts as if he was caught with his hand in the cookie jar. His face immediately turns red, cheeks flush from embarrassment. He grabs a file from his desk, not really knowing or caring about what's inside. He walks past her on his way out of the building and smiles. "I'm headed home now, feel free to call if anything comes up." Mitch is proud that he was able to turn the situation around and put their focus back on business.

"No problem, but I should be alright." She grins at him, her rose colored lips separating just enough to allow her teeth to show. Her hair swings behind her head as she turns around and sits down at her desk. "Have a good night."

## *Chapter 5*

The sound from his alarm throws Mitch into a panic. It's not that he has woken up at an extremely early hour, which is the best benefit of having the title that he does, it's more the feeling that his body has not had ample time to rest. It's only eight but he feels as if he barely slept a wink. He remembers flipping through the television channels hoping to find something to take his mind off the female deputy and her flirtatious ways. He had very little success and ended up falling asleep with an old western on the screen.

Following a quick shower, Mitch fires up his truck and heads for his usual spot to get his morning coffee and breakfast. Maddie's Diner is the only place to get a real cup of coffee in town, unless you count the trendy shops that pop up in the summer to cater to the tourists. It's still early enough in the morning that he can drive straight through the red light in the center of town, another fringe benefit of the job. He hangs a sharp left into the parking lot on the side of the building, walks around the corner and enters the diner.

Maddie's Diner consists of a long counter, with low stools for patrons to sit on. On the opposite wall, there are about five booth style tables, for groups wanting to sit together. Mitch does a quick search of the counter and sees a familiar face with an open stool next to him. He sits at this same counter almost every morning and he has never seen Deputy Jerome Carter here before.

"Deputy Carter, how are we this morning?" The sheriff rests his hat on the counter and smiles at the waitress as she drops off a menu for him. The same waitress delivers a menu to him just about every morning, but Mitch can't remember the last time he opened it.

"Sheriff, I didn't expect to see you. I'm just getting some nourishment in me in case we have to trek back out to the creek today." Jerome shoves the last bite of toast into his mouth after speaking.

"That's probably a good idea. Mind if we have a talk? I haven't really had a chance to get to know you much." After the events of Graham Park, it was a mad scramble to find at least one more officer to join the force. Mitch was relieved when he got a call from Agent Walker from the F.B.I. stating that he had an agent who was having some issues and needed to relocate. "You got here right at the start of the busy season. Things got very hectic and I don't really know much about you."

Deputy Carter adjusts himself in his seat to present his over-sized body in a more upright position. The man is well over six feet tall and has spent his fair share of time lifting weights. He is an impressive figure to look at, not to mention that the people in this area aren't really used to seeing a black guy in town. Mitch never worried about the color of a person's skin, but he knows several people in town who might. He remembers having a conversation with Jerome about this very subject when he first showed up at the station. "I'm not afraid of these small-town hicks" was the exact response he gave to the sheriff. Carter comes across as a tough guy, he rarely smiles and walks around as if he is mad at the world.

"You can ask me anything you want Sheriff, I have never been good at hiding things from people. I guess that's part of the reason why I'm down here in your lovely village." He rolls his eyes at the last statement making it obvious that he is not fond of the small town, lovely or not. "Back in Portland I had issues with the people up the chain of command. I voiced my concerns and now I'm here. I wasn't given much of a say in the matter. I guess that's it in a nutshell."

Mitch takes a moment to ponder what Carter just told him, tells the waitress he'll have his usual and adds a little sugar to his coffee. "Seems pretty legit to me. How are things at the office? How are you getting along with Johnson and Nichols?" Mitch knows more than he is being told from Carter, but he elects to keep his cards close to his chest.

"Stuart is an odd bird, but I get along with him alright. As far as Sloane goes, let's just say I'm trying to keep my distance. She is one feisty woman." Again, he must reposition his body, this time swinging his left leg around to the other side of the stool. "If I didn't know any better, I would think she had the hots for everyone she talks to. I guess that's just how some women talk, but man, it can be too much for me sometimes. It seems like she is either flirting with you, or ready to kick your butt."

Mitch nods in agreement and reaches for his cell phone in his pocket. As he pulls it out the ringer is far louder than he expected, and he fumbles over the buttons before answering it. He responds with a few groans of approval and heads out the door to speak in private. Deputy Carter is left at the counter alone, but he pays little attention to the sheriff. He has been kept out of the loop on matters before, it is standard operating procedure in the F.B.I.

"Don't worry, I'll be there in two minutes." He slams the phone shut and heads back into the diner. After throwing a ten on the counter, he gives Carter a look to let him know the message relayed to him on the phone was not good. "We need to get to the station immediately. It looks like someone left us a little present this morning."

**Kevin M. Moehring**

## *Chapter 6*

His heart is racing. The feeling is very similar to how he felt three months ago, when the lights of the Ferris Wheel pierced the dark night sky. He runs up the steps and into the police station, finding Nichols and Johnson standing at the counter with a cardboard box in between them. He races to the other side of the counter, nods at the two deputies before beginning to examine the box and its contents.

"Where did you find this?" He aims the question at Nichols, who has been here all night, but instead he hears the deeper voice of Stuart Johnson. The senior officer tells him that it was just sitting on the top step when he came in to work. The flaps to the box are still closed, showing the message on the outside. There is nothing else remarkable about the box, it's just a typical moving box with the written message on the top.

*YOU DIDN'T SAVE THEM THEN*

*YOU CAN'T SAVE THEM NOW*

The message is written with a large black marker, much how a person would label a box prior to putting it on the moving truck. The letters are legible but have the appearance of being written by a child. Mitch reaches into one of the drawers behind the counter and pulls out a pair of latex gloves. As he slides them on, he can't help the feeling of fear that has begun to creep through his body. He made certain that the other two officers did not open the box before he got there. Much like his father, he takes the role as sheriff to mean that he is the one to be put in harm's way far before anyone else.

Deputy Carter slides into the room and stands on the opposite side of the counter, observant yet silent. Mitch pulls out his pocket knife and carefully slices along the seam of the box, splitting the tape and allowing the flaps to rise slightly. As his knife easily slices through the final piece of tape, he notices the other deputies all take a step or two away from the counter. He looks at them, thinking that if they were afraid that there was an explosive of some kind inside, the few feet they just retreated would not be nearly enough to keep them safe.

Using the end of a pencil to pry back the first side of the cardboard, Mitch himself is relieved that nothing happens. Even after everything that he went through a few months ago, he is still a bit unclear as to what dangers the world holds. It's easy to become complacent when you don't deal with the same problems as the larger cities on a daily basis. Confident that the box will not explode, he uses the same pencil to fold back the opposite side.

With the box now open and the contents exposed, Mitch is left breathless and at a loss for words. The others all move in closer, so they can see what gift had been left for them on the front steps. Once he gets sight of the contents of the box, Stuart Johnson heads straight for the garbage can to empty out his stomach. He has never been fond of gore or seeing blood, both of which he sees inside the box. Carter has the most experience of the group in dealing with serious crimes, and he studies the contents closely, moving his head around so he can see everything from as many angles as possible, surely a technique that comes straight from the F.B.I. handbook.

After cleaning the remaining vomit from his face with a napkin, Stuart breaks the silence by mentioning the obvious. "That's two hands. Someone sent us two bloody hands in a box."

The other three officers fail to respond or even acknowledge that Stuart said anything at all. Instead they are staring at the hands resting in the box with wide eyes. The fingers of each hand are laced together, as if they are a young couple in love holding hands as they walk in the park.

"Alright, let's start throwing our observations out loud so we can all have as much intel about this as possible. It's obvious that these come from two different people, one being a male and the other a female." Mitch is hoping that by starting the conversation, it will allow the others to chime in with whatever information they find about the body parts.

"There's a gold ring on the female hand," comes from the high-pitched voice of Nichols. "It's not a wedding or an engagement ring, but it is valuable enough to hold some meaning to the woman."

Carter has already pulled out his cell phone and started taking pictures. "The wound on both hands is crisp and clean. It would have been a quick cut with a sharp object. Probably something bigger than a knife."

Mitch hadn't noticed the cleanliness with which the hands had been cut from the bodies. He had been caught up in looking at the ring that Sloane had mentioned and had not even considered finding any evidence from the wound itself. "Something bigger than a knife? You have the most experience dealing with things like this Carter but tell me why you think the weapon would be bigger than a knife."

Carter walks around the counter and stands between the sheriff and Nichols. He pulls a pen from his chest pocket and uses it to point at the severed end of the hands, opposite where the fingers are positioned together. "First of all, it looks like the hands were removed in a single blow. There are no chips in the bone from previous failed attempts and if a knife was used to saw through the bone, the result would be much more jagged. I'm no expert but I'm guessing the person who did this used a very sharp tool with a handle. A meat clever or maybe even an..."

"I know what you're going to say but let's just stop right there before we jump to any conclusions." After the calls that were received at the station yesterday, the last thing Mitch wants to hear about is another man with an axe. "Anyone else see anything worth mentioning about what's in here?"

There is a prolonged period of silence. Each officer is looking into the box, looking for any evidence that they can be the first to see. Nobody speaks up until Sheriff Thompson begins giving out orders. "Stuart, you have the best knowledge of the computer system. I need you to get the prints from these hands and run them through the database." Stuart instantly turns his nose up at the thought of having to touch the bloody hands.

"Carter, since you have the most knowledge of how they operate, I want you to take the contents of the box to your friends in Portland. See if you can get some of your buddies at the F.B.I. to run a few tests. Get anything you can from the trace evidence and let me know what you find out." Deputy Carter has no desire to return to Portland as a defeated man, having to face the very agents who asked him to leave town, especially since he will need their help.

"Nichols, you should probably head home. You've been on-duty all night and need to get some sleep. When you're rested, come on back and check in with me. I'm sure there will be plenty to do." Mitch looks at the female officer and can tell that she is not a fan of what he has asked her to do.

"I've been here for over a month and the most excitement I've had is arresting the naked man who had a little extra before leaving the Bottom Dollar. Now that we get a real case, you want me to leave and get some sleep?" The tone of her voice is completely different from what any of the men have heard her use in the past. The words come out with force, as if she is going to begin spitting fire as well.

"Right now, the only thing we can do is investigate. I'm going to pull the footage from the cameras out front. Those things are never lit well enough, but maybe we can see who left us the box. It's going to take hours for Carter to hear anything from the feds and maybe even longer before we get a match on the prints." Trying to convince a woman to do something she doesn't want to do is not an art form that the young sheriff has had any practice with, and it shows in the way he is speaking to her.

For a brief instance, there is no response from Deputy Nichols, just a shaking of her head. Carter and Johnson can feel the intensity and carry the box away to get started on what they were asked to do. Once the other two men leave the room, Sloane changes her mood and a wry smile crosses her face. The redness leaves her cheeks almost as fast as it appeared.

"How about I brew a new pot of coffee, and we watch the tapes together. If two eyes are better than one, then how good are four eyes going to be? I'll even change out of my uniform so that I won't look like I'm working."

# *Chapter 7*

Mitch Thompson returns to the safety and solitude of his office. He collapses into his seat as if the weight of the world had just been dropped onto his broad shoulders. A knock at his door draws his attention and without prompting Lucille Pennington walks in. Mitch hadn't seen her come in, but he imagines she just took a seat at her desk by the front door while they were looking at the box. She has been at the station long enough to know when to be invisible.

"Good morning Sheriff, Mayor Billings is on hold for you." She shuffles about the room and leaves a few papers on his desk. She must be the least curious woman in the world, as she never even asks what all the commotion is about.

"Take a message for me. He is always getting on me if I don't check in with him first thing in the morning." He looks up at the woman and gives her a smile, which she ignores and heads for the door. "Thanks Lucille."

Mitch turns his attention to the computer on his desk which has access to every camera in the building, as well as the ones on the exterior of the brick structure. A few taps of the keys and he has pulled up the four screens that show every corner of the building. He decides to watch the rear facing camera first, knowing that there is going to be nothing to find on the recording. He uses various buttons to fast forward through most of the night. There appears to be no change on the image other than a few headlights shining through.

Before he can begin the second video, he waves to Carter as he heads out of the building. He's carrying the box, severed hands still inside, under his arm like a running back in a football game. Mitch wonders if Stuart would have carried the box the same way or if the older deputy would have held it out from his body hoping to avoid the smell. As the front door to the station closes, Mitch catches a glimpse of Deputy Nichols, who has indeed changed out of her uniform and back into the yoga pants and sports bra she was wearing when he saw her the day before. He takes in the entirety of her body; her long legs, her tight abs and skin that is naturally a few shades darker than his own. Her body is perfectly proportioned and well-toned, surely a result of extensive exercise. He decides he may need to start a petition to outlaw this kind of attire in the work place.

When she opens the door to his office, he snaps his eyes back to the computer monitor. As if invited to do so, she pulls a chair behind his desk and takes up a position on his right side. How a person can work a twelve-hour shift and change into clothes from the day before, and still smell this amazing is a mystery to Mitch. It's a struggle for him to focus on the task at hand, hitting multiple keys in error instead of the single one that would start the video.

Several minutes go by, the two of them sitting in silence and staring at the same screen. They are watching the front of the building now, the concrete steps at the bottom of the screen. There isn't much to see unless you count a few birds sitting on the overhang and the cars that race past. A few more minutes go by and the traffic is all but gone on the street. The image becomes lighter as the sun begins to rise. Mitch is beginning to get angry that the security system they have in place is not good enough to catch whoever left them the package.

"Wait! Stop the video!" Sloane Nichols sits upright and moves to the edge of her seat. "Go back a little. I think I saw something."

Mitch hits a few buttons and rewinds the video, hits play and waits. Again, his irritation rises as they see nothing for several seconds with the video playing in regular speed. Suddenly from the bottom right-hand side of the screen, a dark figure moves in. You can see the person carrying the box, leaving it on the top step and racing away. The whole thing took less than five seconds, and whoever it was moved quickly and fluidly.

Mitch rewinds the tape again and stops it at the appropriate spot. It takes just a few seconds for the figure to enter the screen again. This time, when the shadow is on the top step dropping off the box, Mitch hits the pause button. They both lean into the screen, trying to get as good of a look at it as they can. The poor image quality makes it difficult for either of them to see anything. He can feel her breath on the side of his face, causing the tiny hairs on his neck to stand up.

"There, on his back! Is that what I think it is?" Mitch points to the middle of the screen to show her exactly what he is pointing at.

"I'm not sure what you think it is Sheriff, but to me it looks like an axe," she responds.

"I need to print this, so we can see it on paper, maybe that will give us a clearer image of the object." Mitch begins to push a few buttons, even though he is not sure how to accomplish what he wants.

"Mitch, if you allow me to get in there, I can probably help. We can save the video file and send it out to be enhanced. It might take some time, but I have some friends down in L.A. who are film editors and could help us." This is the first time that he can recall when she called him by his first name. Maybe she did it on purpose to try to gain his trust or maybe she just got caught up in the fact that they found some evidence. Either way, he liked it.

He looks at her with an odd look. The look you give someone when you find out something important about them for the first time. He realizes that he doesn't know very much about her, let alone what kind of friends she had before she came to town. The fact that she has intimidated him with her looks since day one has been an ongoing struggle for him since she was hired.

"How long will that take? I want to see what that is on the person's back right away." It's times like these that he wished he had a better knowledge of computers and current technology. The fact is that all the electronics they currently have, including the cameras that caught the image, were gifts from the feds in Portland. Apparently, Agent Walker thought they needed to catch up to the times a bit.

She uses her elbow to nudge him aside and muscles her way in front of the keyboard. "It's going to take longer if you don't get out of my way and let me do my thing."

It has been quite a while since Mitch has been made to feel useless, and he has never been made to feel that way by a woman. He watches over her for a moment, speechless and intrigued. She focuses on the screen and her fingers move quickly over the keyboard. He's not sure what it is, but there is something special about that woman.

# *Chapter 8*

Mitch stands behind Stuart Johnson as names and mugshots scroll quickly on the computer screen. They are waiting for the results from the fingerprint scan that they performed on the two hands they found in the box. Neither man has any idea how long a search like this typically takes. They have never had the need to use the new computer equipment since they got it a couple of months ago. After the Graham Park incident, the F.B.I. insisted upon helping with the improvement of the technology at the station and Stuart is the only person who attended the training class in Portland that taught the basics of using the machines.

Deputy Carter probably knows more about the technology than anyone else in the department, but Mitch feels confident that he made the right call when he sent the former agent to Portland with the box and bloody hands. They wait patiently trying to catch glimpses of faces as they cycle through. The program has been running for well over an hour and shows no signs of stopping any time soon. Sheriff Thompson decides to leave Stuart alone at the computer and return to his own office where he left Deputy Nichols.

"Just in time Sheriff. My friend sent back a clearer image of the person who left us the package. Come here and have a look for yourself." She looks up at him from his chair, confident and proud, yet not smug.

Mitch moves in behind the female deputy and stands over her. He expected that she would get up from his desk when he got there, but she stayed seated. He bends down, his face inches from hers, and peers at the image on the screen. It is indeed much clearer than what they saw on the grainy footage from the camera. Sloane clicks through several images, going back and forth between three of the ones that show glimpses of the person's face. It is a male figure, but his long hair and bushy beard makes it hard to see much of his face at all.

"Not much to see there. Do we have any better images of what he's carrying?" He says these words in a whisper, realizing that his mouth is very close to her ear as they look at the screen side by side.

A few clicks of the mouse later and the object on the man's back becomes clearer. He has no idea how the people enhanced the images and made them this clean, but he is happy with the results. All he knows is that now he can clearly see that the person has a long axe strapped to his back. An axe would be a loose description in Mitch's opinion. The weapon looks medieval, with both sides of the head of the axe containing a sharp edge. He determines it must have been made by the man carrying it, knowing that there would be no practical need for an axe with the cutting edge on both sides of the blade. The handle itself looks like it is nothing more than a tree branch that had been whittled down to fit nicely in the palm of a hand.

"Print these off and bring them over to Stuart's desk. I want him to get a look at them and see if he recognizes the face. Hopefully he'll get a hit on the prints soon enough. I'm going to call Tom Blevins and see if his missing couple has turned up." He leaves Deputy Nichols to her duties and heads to the front counter to find the form that was filled out the night before, the one with the phone number for the campground owner. He gives the old man a call and is not happy to hear that the couple in question had still not turned up. Mitch adds the name of the man who rented the cabin to the form, but Mr. Blevins was unable to provide a name for the female.

The three deputies have gathered near Stuart's desk, looking over the enhanced pictures hoping something will catch their eye or trigger a clue as to who the man is. The computer on the desk is still hard at work trying to match the fingerprints they lifted from the two hands. Mitch knows what the next course of action should be, and he is dreading the inevitable hiking trip along Hidden Creek. All the callers yesterday claim they saw the man with the axe along the creek, and Mr. Blevins said that's where the hikers were heading when they left the camp. That would be the most likely spot to begin the investigation and start looking for this man with the hand-made axe.

Satisfied that the pictures are not jarring the memory of any of the deputies, Mitch gathers them up and sticks them in his pocket. "Stuart, you stay here and wait for a match of some kind. Deputy Nichols and I are going on a little hiking trip."

# *Chapter 9*

Mitch waits in his truck for Sloane to finish putting on her uniform once again. There are a million thoughts running through his head and he's not sure what makes him more uncomfortable, the man with the axe running through the woods or being alone with Nichols on the drive to Hidden Creek. The young sheriff has never experienced the feelings he gets whenever he is around her, the nauseating pain in his stomach that feels like his insides could burst at any moment. For the last three years, he has done little socializing, except for his nightly visits to the bar where he prefers to sit alone and talk to no one. He wonders if Nichols really has feelings for him or if he is imagining the way she looks at him to be more than it really is. Maybe she isn't doing it intentionally or maybe she is deliberately messing with his head.

He is snapped back to reality with the opening of his passenger door and the smile she gives him as she climbs in. "You sure you're going to be able to keep up with me out there in the woods?"

For a moment, Mitch forgot where they were supposed to be going, "I've spent my fair share of time hiking along that creek. The terrain is tough, but I think I can manage." He is amazed at the way she looks and smells, with no lasting signs that she worked a long shift overnight. Her eyes look normal and she is just as energetic as she is every other day when she begins her shift.

It takes nearly twenty minutes to reach the clearing where cars park whenever hikers dare to challenge themselves with a trek along the creek. The two officers drove the entire length in silence, Mitch focusing on keeping the truck in the center of his lane as the road snaked along. Sloane paid more attention to her cell phone, surely keeping up to date with social media. She has been in town long enough to understand the limits of cell phone service and wants to get in as much time as she can before her phone turns into an overpriced clock. As the sheriff heads to the rear of his truck to begin changing his shoes, out of the cowboy boots and into a more appropriate pair of hunting boots, Nichols has begun a stretching exercise. He tries not to look but is captivated by the way she effortlessly bends at the waist and places her palms on the ground. Even in the less than flattering uniform pants, Mitch can still make out the firmness of her body.

They drove the extra five minutes to begin their part of the hike at the far west end of their jurisdiction. Before leaving the station, he gave instructions for Stuart to ride along with Carter when he got back from Portland and for them to start at the eastern end of the creek and start working their way west. Mitch is hoping that the two groups would be able to meet somewhere in the middle, which would cut down the amount of hiking each pair had to do.

Hidden Creek gets its name because it sits in a valley, far below the road on the south side and the hills to the north. Most people drive along Highway 30 and have no idea that all the twists and turns in the road are a result of the creek that sits below. The forest is thickest in this area and along both sides of the creek is a large section of gravel and dirt. Amateur hikers find the steep hills and loose footing far too difficult to navigate, meaning not many tourists come hiking in this area except for the more advanced explorers.

Mitch and Sloane begin to make their descents down the hillside. They face each other, extending one leg down the hill before moving the second leg down to meet it. She looks at him from time to time to make sure that he is not getting too far in front of her. Mitch feels rushed, moving quicker than he normally would as to not let her beat him down the hill. Moving forward hesitantly, they remain focused on firm footing and trying not to look too far in front of them. Each step has its own set of obstacles. Everything from loose rocks, trash that has been thrown out of cars along the highway and broken tree branches slow their progress.

Mitch has used this same footwork technique several times over the years, usually on hunting trips into the woods with his father. Sloane looks like a natural, which is a shock considering she spent most of her life in the big city. Her movements are fluid and she gains confidence with each stride. He can tell that Deputy Nichols is a naturally athletic woman by the way her body moves and the ease with which she is handling the rough terrain. The humidity has caused both officers to begin to sweat. Mitch has soiled his shirt completely by the time they reach the bottom of the hill and the pair take a moment to gather their breath on the shoreline. He tries to mask his fatigue, refusing to put his hands behind his head to improve his breathing. He doesn't want to look weak in front of Sloane, who appears no worse for the wear.

Since Mitch has the waterproof boots on, it is decided that he will be the one to cross the creek and examine the opposite side. Hidden Creek is only twelve feet across at its widest spot and rarely is it more than a couple of feet deep. Mitch manages to find enough large rocks to step on and avoid getting his pants wet any higher up than his ankles. Once on the other side, he begins to motion at Deputy Nichols in hand gestures, which they had worked out prior to separating. He motions with his fingers as if they were walking on their own across a table or desk and points down the creek. The two head east, back in the direction of town, both hoping to find nothing but telling themselves they probably will.

**Kevin M. Moehring**

## *Chapter 10*

They have been walking along the creek for nearly thirty minutes and have yet to find anything. There were times when one of them would throw their hand up, telling the other that they may have found something. In these instances, all they found was an empty water bottle or a wrapper from an energy bar. It amazes Mitch that so many people travel to this area to take in nature and the beauty of the area and then seem to do their best at trashing it. The sun is at its highest point now, just high enough in the sky to shine the rays through the trees and straight down on the two officers. In their long-sleeved uniforms and with it being in the middle of July, they are drinking their small water supply much more quickly than they should.

Just ahead of them, the creek makes a sharp turn toward the right. The gravel and dirt seem to disappear behind the steep hill that acts as a wall, holding back the forest and trees to allow the creek to flow freely. Sheriff Thompson is the first to make the turn at the bend in the creek, thus being the first to spot the body that is hanging above the water. He races ahead, hearing the footsteps of his female partner matching him in pace. His feet hit the small rocks loud enough that anyone in the area would know that he was there. The sound echoes off the sides of the surrounding hills, hanging in the air for what seems like an eternity.

Deputy Nichols must have been moving far faster than the sheriff had. She has already crossed the creek and is standing next to him as he looks up at the body that seems to be floating above the water. The ankles are bound by a long piece of rope that extends to a large pine tree about twenty feet up the side of the hill on Mitch's side of the creek. The arms are also tied in similar fashion with the rope secured to another large tree halfway up the hill on what was Sloane's side of the creek. The body hangs only a few feet above the water, like a human piñata that is waiting to spill its bloody contents into the waiting water below.

The anxiety has returned in the young sheriff, the exact feeling he felt when he saw the lights on the Ferris

Wheel spinning a few months earlier. He has studied several books about proper police protocol since becoming the head man, but now that he is faced with a body hanging from a couple of trees, fear has taken over his body and he is unable to think clearly. He's not sure what to do. This is not something they cover in the police manuals and he never thought it would be something that would happen in Twisted Timbers. His first instinct is to cut the body down, but he quickly decides the body would land in the water and make it impossible to find any trace evidence that may have been left behind. He scrambles through the loads of information stored in his mind, trying to find something that will let him know how to handle the situation. He finds nothing.

Sloane is not as frozen in place as Mitch is, moving closer to the body and inspecting the water beneath it. She is standing in the middle of the creek, surely drenched from the knee down. She has her phone out, snapping pictures of everything she finds to be relevant. "Sheriff, you need to see this. Looks like our killer has sent us another message."

Mitch jumps at the sound of her voice; the silence of the forest being broken unexpectedly. He moves into the water and stands next to her, feeling the warm water rise to the middle of his legs. The two officers stare up at the body, like two lovers watching the stars in the night sky. "I see it too. It looks like this man is probably the owner of the hand that was in our box." It didn't take much police work to notice the stub on the end of the dead man's hand.

"That's not really what I was talking about. Look at his chest," she points above her to where the man's shirt has been ripped open. There are three large letters carved into the man's skin. Each letter is made by making three long slices into the flesh, or with three blows from an axe. The letters are written individually, starting at the top of the chest, near the throat, and ending near the belly button. They are large block letters, each one outlined in the dark red color of the blood that has dripped from the wounds.

The fear inside of him has increased and once he realizes what the letters are trying to tell them, his heart races faster still. Even though he has never been good at solving riddles or word puzzles, he knows that the three letters on the man's chest mean that they are in danger. There is no other meaning for the letters, there is nothing else that the killer could be trying to tell them. The letters I, C and U can only mean one thing to Mitch and his deputy. It means someone is watching them and knows that they are in these woods alone.

**Kevin M. Moehring**

## *Chapter 11*

The two officers have taken up shelter under a tall tree near where the shoreline meets the hills. The root of the massive oak is somewhat exposed, probably due to a portion of the hillside giving way and falling into the creek. After reading the message that had been carved into the hanging man's chest, they both had the uneasy feeling of being watched. While sitting on the hard ground, Mitch has been trying to reach either Johnson or Carter and try to let them know what was going on. His calls would initially go through, but as soon as someone would answer on the other end, the call would disconnect. This is not uncommon in this area, but it doesn't make it any less of a nuisance either.

From what he could piece together, the remaining two deputies have made their way to the creek and have begun their hike west. The plan was for Mitch and Nichols to cover most of the ground before the other two made it to the creek. That plan has since changed thanks to the dead body hanging above the water. He knows that eventually someone is going to have to cut the body down. He also knows that now is not a good time for him to be hiking through these woods to get to where the ropes are attached to the trees, being as there is someone out here that has bad intentions. He comes up with a plan, to stay put where they are and wait for the other two deputies to show up. This will make getting the body down much easier and will allow for one of the four to always keep an eye on their surroundings while the others do the work.

It has been a half an hour since they found the body. The two have not spoken a word since they moved under the tree branches, hoping the silence would give away the location of the killer and keep them hidden. So far, they have not heard a sound, other than the running water of the creek. They had finished off the last of their water about five minutes ago, and Mitch is wondering how he should go about filling the canteen. He knows the water in the creek is potable, having drunk from it many times in his youth. However, he also knows that blood from the body has been dripping into the creek for an unknown amount of time.

He has no way of knowing if there are other bodies further up the creek. He also has no way of knowing how long the two may be stuck here, waiting for Johnson and Carter. Mitch still doesn't know much about Deputy Carter, but he has known Stuart long enough to know that he suffers from a severe case of Murphy's Law, so waiting on the men might not be the best option. He decides it is in their best interest to fill the canteen from the water that has yet to pass under the body. To do this, Mitch is going to have to leave the security of the massive root where they have been hiding. Without saying a word, he motions to Sloane his intentions, shaking the canteen and pointing at himself and then the creek. She nods that she understands what he intends to do and unholsters her police issued pistol. She holds it out in front of her body, reminiscent of a Charlie's Angels pose, and gives him a nod of assurance.

He rises to his feet slowly, slightly bent at the waist to avoid hitting the branches overhead. He can feel his muscles are tight, from the exertion of the hike followed immediately by the prolonged period of sitting and not moving. His eyes dart from side to side, looking for any sign of life among the trees. He slowly makes his way along the tree line, under the rope that is holding the dead man's feet, to the other side of the creek where he is sure the water has not been soiled with the blood from the hanging man. Mitch stays as close to the hillside as he can, just in case the killer is on the same side of the creek as they have been hiding. The sheriff is hoping that is the case because to fill the canteen, he will need to cover the twelve feet of bank quickly and will have no cover to protect him. If he has succeeded in avoiding detection until he makes his move toward the water, it may give him the time he needs to fill the canteen and return to safety before the killer can make a move.

He pauses for a minute, looks up and down the creek, checks the opposite hill for anything out of the ordinary and looks back at Deputy Nichols. She looks appealing with her weapon drawn. Mitch wonders if it is the firepower in her hands that turns him on or the confidence she shows while holding it. Either way, looking at her has almost made him forget about the current situation. He unscrews the lid to the canteen, hoping it will save him time while he is in the open and near the creek. After a long inhale, he takes several long, quick strides and reaches the water.

While the bubbles indicate that the water is filling the metal canteen, he takes the time to look at the hill that he has been unable to see since taking cover. The trees are so thick that it is unlikely that he would be able to see anyone, even if they were wearing brightly colored clothes. If this was happening in the fall, when most of the trees have lost their colorful leaves, it would be far easier to spot someone who was perched on the higher ground. By all indications, the person they have been chasing, or hiding from, has only been seen wearing nothing but black attire. That limits the chances he will be spotted if he is nestled in among the pine trees and the dark shadows that they create.

Confident that he has gotten as much water as he could, Mitch quickly screws on the lid, shoves the canteen into his front pocket and begins making his way back to the shelter of the trees. He isn't running now, thinking that if there was someone in the woods, they would have taken their shot at him while he was near the water. He looks down at Nichols once more, her head is on a swivel with weapon leading the way, blonde locks flailing behind her head with every turn.

He feels a bump near his pocket, but his senses are drawn more to the sound of her voice calling out his name. She yells out for him, much in a manner of a mother yelling for a lost child. He is not sure what has happened, but now he can feel the sensation of something wet running down his side. Thoughts are racing through his mind, wondering if he has been shot, wondering why he doesn't feel any pain. He looks down at his hip and notices an arrow is sticking out of his side. That must have been the bump that he felt right before Sloane called out his name. "That must be what I feel running down my side, it's my own blood," he mutters to himself.

# *Chapter 12*

The arrow sticks out from his side like a piece of equipment that he added to his waistband before heading into the woods. The canteen that absorbed the impact from the arrow is now bone dry and any hope of getting more water is dashed. He tugs the projectile from his side and drops it on the ground, relieved that the sharp tip did not penetrate his skin. The thought that someone has fired an arrow in his direction was a bit odd at first, but finally panic sets in and sends him sprawling across the rocky bank as fast as he can move. When he reaches Deputy Nichols, he dives head first to hide under the safety of the tree root and watches as she waves her pistol from side to side trying to focus on a target. He can tell that she has no idea where the shot came from, her gun is moving faster than her eyes can keep up with.

On the opposite side of the creek, the rustling of the trees makes it clear that something is moving on the ridge, but they have been unable to get a look at the person. Mitch struggles to catch his breath and Sloane gives up her hunt and turns her attention to the sheriff. The person who shot the arrow must have been waiting for the perfect shot for a long time, as neither of them noticed any sign of movement for the whole time they were held up under the safety of the large tree. Now that Sloane is confident that the shooter has fled the area, she feels it's safe enough to return her weapon to its holster. Her cheeks are red and for the first time all day, beads of sweat have formed near her hairline.

Mitch stands to his feet and removes the once full canteen from his front pocket. The arrow that pierced through the side has left a puncture hole in the perfect form of a circle. Luckily, the resistance from the water prevented the projectile from going through the other side of the metal container, thus saving his thigh from any damage. He is relieved to have not been hit directly and feels even better when he sees the look of relief in the eye of his fellow officer. She looks up at him with flush cheeks and eyes spread wide in disbelief. When the arrow was protruding from his side, she must have thought that it had found its target and gone into his leg. Now that they are both finding out that the canteen stopped it from doing any damage, a slight smile comes across her face. Not a smile that shows she finds the outcome funny at all, but more of a smile of relief.

She rises to her feet and the two look at each other. Her eyes are a deep shade of blue that he can feel stare right through his soul. He wonders if he is the only one who is feeling the obvious attraction between them. He wonders if now would be the right time to make a move and lean in for a kiss. He refrains, deciding instead to dust off his pants and clear the dirt from his uniform, diverting his eyes away from hers. Somewhere in the back of his mind he can hear his father reminding him to make sure not to crap where you eat. He is surprised when he looks up and she has her pistol pointed right at him. For a brief second, he fears that Sloane has somehow pieced together what Mitch had been thinking in the moments prior. It takes a second or two for him to realize that she has it pointed over his shoulder to the area behind him.

He follows her stare and turns around to face away from her and down the creek. There is movement and sounds coming from the east, the sound of rocks rolling and feet hitting the granite stones echoes through the valley. Mitch is barely able to reach his pistol and aim it in the appropriate direction before he realizes that the footsteps he hears are coming from Johnson and Carter. The two deputies are racing along the same side of the creek and pick up the pace as they see Sheriff Thompson and Deputy Nichols. Not only is Mitch glad to see them because he wants the extra manpower, but them being here also relieves the stress he feels from being alone with Deputy Nichols.

"Sheriff, is everything alright? We heard someone scream and we took off in this direction." Stuart Johnson is almost out of breath by the time he reaches the spot under the tree. His pant legs are still rolled up to his knees, an obvious attempt to keep them dry while crossing the creek. Sloane lets out a giggle at the sight of the man with his white legs showing between his pants leg and dark socks.

"Everything is fine. We have been waiting here for you guys to show up. We found this body hanging up here and didn't want to leave it out here unprotected." Sheriff Thompson points in the direction of the body that has been hanging over the creek since they discovered it an hour ago. "Since then, the circumstances have changed. Protecting the body is no longer our top priority." He explains to the two officers what happened when he tried to fill the canteen and points out where they saw the rustling of the trees.

"I think I might have a good idea as to who that is hanging up there. It took a while for a match to come back on the prints we ran, for a top of the line computer system, that thing sure is slow. The male hand belongs to a Robert Eldridge out of Seattle. He was in the system for a DUI a couple of years back. We got no match on the prints from the female hand." Stuart seems to be impressed with the knowledge the computer produced and the fact that he could be the first to give the sheriff the news.

Sheriff Thompson nods that he understands what Stuart has just told him. "That name is the same one that I got when I talked to Tom Blevins. I wanted to make sure the hand belonged to the missing man before we made any assumptions." He then turns his attention to Jerome Carter who showed up a few steps behind Stuart. The look he gives the newer deputy says he is waiting to hear anything he could find out from his former friends in Portland when he took the hands to the F.B.I. offices.

"Well, there wasn't much they could tell me right away except that the weapon used to make the cut was definitely bigger than a knife and very sharp. They agreed with our assumption that it looked like the cuts were made from a single blow, probably from an axe." Jerome stops long enough to pull out his cell phone, press the button to check the screen and return it to his pocket. "They told me they would run tests on them right away and let me know as soon as they had anything, but I hadn't heard anything up until I lost reception."

Mitch was hoping to find out the identity of both hands that were dropped on the doorstep of the police station as well as getting a little more information from the forensics folks in Portland. Unfortunately, they were not able to add much to the investigation other than a meaningless name to go along with the body that is hanging over Hidden Creek. They are no further along in finding out who the person is that is hiding in the woods and shooting arrows at them. They are also no further along in figuring out how to find this person and keep the hiking trails in the area safe for the tourists that have flooded the area. If the mayor catches wind of what is going on, Mitch will never be able to keep him off his back.

# Evil in the Woods

Having all four members of the police force now in the middle of the woods is not ideal. Mitch didn't factor this in when he told the other two officers to meet him here when they finished with the tasks he had given them. Hopefully there isn't anything too pressing that happens in town before one of them can get back to the station and assist Lucille. Mitch also didn't factor in that someone would be out here firing wooden arrows at his thighs. Either way, they are all here and they must do their duty and pursue the suspect. He knows that Stuart will be up to the task, having grown up in this area and being familiar with the terrain makes up for anything lost by his advanced age.

Carter and Nichols, on the other hand, have no experience in the woods and come from much larger cities. If the team is going to chase after a suspect who obviously feels very comfortable in the forest, these two officers may need a little assistance. Mitch decides they will need to split into two teams and search on separate sides of the creek. Due to their lack of outdoor experience and survival skills, Nichols will stay with Mitch and Carter and Johnson will hike across the creek. This way Mitch can be sure that the new deputies are both paired with someone who has spent far more time in the woods than they have. Being alone with Sloane adds unneeded pressure on the shoulders of Mitch, but he can't pass up the opportunity to spend more time alone with the woman. Teaming with Sloane during the investigation is far more appealing to Mitch than walking through the woods with either Johnson or Carter.

Mitch takes a minute to point out the things they have learned about the suspended body of Robert Eldridge, then tells Johnson and Carter to investigate the side of the creek where they currently stand. He knew the shot came from the other side and he wouldn't be able to live with himself if he knowingly sent Stuart to the side of the creek where the shot came from and something happened to the older officer. He motions to Nichols and watches her gracefully hop from one stone to another as she crosses the creek and lands on the dry ground on the other side. Like a young boy on a playground, he chases after her.

# *Chapter 13*

His father always warned him of the dangers of the woods but of all the things he warned him of, a man shooting arrows was never mentioned. Much as he has done for the last few months, Mitch is learning on the fly. He has yet to come across a handbook or manual that would teach him how to hunt down someone in the thick forest where he currently finds himself, but he is certain it wouldn't be of much use to him now. Not only is he trying to figure things out as he goes along, he is also responsible for the well-being of the other three officers, a responsibility that he takes seriously.

He has followed Nichols up the side of the hill, watching intently as she confidently climbs over the fallen branches and large rocks. Now that they have reached the ridge that overlooks the creek, Mitch takes a moment to look across and see that Stuart has also made it up the hill. Deputy Johnson is sitting on a boulder waiting for Carter to make it to the top. Covering terrain like this is a challenge no matter how physically fit a person appears to be. Jerome Carter is a large man, making his footing even more precarious as he tries to dig his feet into the dirt for firm footing. After a few slips and slides, he successfully reaches the top. Stuart and Jerome wave across the creek to the sheriff and disappear into the brush.

Mitch turns to Sloane, taken aback at first that his eyes meet hers, wondering if she has been staring at him this whole time. He takes the lead and heads into the trees, away from Hidden Creek. Every few steps the pair takes, the sheriff stops and looks around. He is vaguely familiar with the area and is hoping to find something that will jar his memory. The feeling is like turning on an old movie and not realizing you have seen it already until a certain scene. He knows they are not far from where the old sawmill was before it burned to the ground. His father talked about the area on several occasions but always warned Mitch to stay away. Of course, Mitch had still been around the area several times, usually with a group of friends. Just because his father was the sheriff doesn't mean that Mitch always listened to him.

He marches forward, using his right foot to clear away a cluster of thickets. Nichols is directly behind him, keeping up without breaking a sweat. Her ability to cover the same terrain as a person who has lived in the area since birth is confusing to the sheriff. As the two power through the thick branches, they find themselves standing on a dirt path. Even though the path is now showing signs of decades of growth and lack of use, Mitch knows right away that it is the access road that leads to the mill.

"This seems like an odd place for a trail," Sloane announces from directly behind Mitch.

"It's not really a trail. The old mill is out here, and this was the access road. It was the only way in or out." Mitch stands in the middle of the road and looks down both sides. The trees have made the road much narrower than it was when it was in use. He reaches for his radio and calls for Stuart, letting the deputy know that he has reached the mill road. Stuart replies that they are still searching the area and will head that way if they don't find anything soon.

"Didn't I hear somewhere that the old mill burned down?" Since Nichols didn't grow up in Twisted

Timbers, she has no knowledge of the mill or the story that surrounded the fire.

"It wasn't long after I was born but I know all about it. Everyone in town knows about it." The story of the sawmill fire is a blemish on the town, one that the town leaders have tried to put behind them for years. "We have about a half mile hike, I'll fill you in on the way."

# *Chapter 14*

Walking side by side down the old mill road is much easier than the hike through the woods. The overhanging trees give much needed shelter from the mid-afternoon sun and there is always a slight breeze. Mitch has been the only one talking up until now, telling Deputy Nichols about the fire that destroyed the sawmill. How it was all blamed on a worker who had been fired and decided the place needed to be destroyed.

Her eyes became teary when he talked about the dozen men who were trapped inside. The entire structure was made from lumber that was produced on-site. In this part of the country, almost everything is made of wood. Once the flames began to spread, there was no way of stopping it. Only two employees made it out of the blaze, and when the police showed up and started taking down their stories, both they could hear the screams coming from inside. According to Mitch's father, burning to death rates at the top of the list of worst ways to die.

Many of the people living in the town still talk about the fire. For several years, they blamed Mitch's father and the Police Department for not acting fast enough. Even though it happened when he was young, Mitch remembers hearing his father talk about the fire on numerous occasions. Of course, everyone in town has their own story about how the fire was started and why the rescue attempts were unsuccessful. Mitch has heard several different versions, each one with a bit of truth but mostly fabrication. The fact is that the mill was in a horrible location, so far from the creek that the water could not be used and too far from town for any rescuers to get to them quickly enough to be of any use.

When he was in school he heard all the same rumors regarding the fire. How the souls of the men who died still haunt the area or how the children of the dead workers still roam the area were usually the favorite topics. Like most of the other ghost stories that are popular in Twisted Timbers, Mitch failed to believe any of it. Every time he would hear a new story, he would run home and ask his father about the validity of it.

Looking back on it now, Mitch is thankful his father was the sheriff of the town and could dismiss the stories, thus allowing Mitch to return to school the next day and set the record straight.

Sloane Nichols has been walking along with Mitch listening to his every word, much as Mitch would listen to his father when he was younger. She is not only paying attention to him, but she's hanging on every word. The sheriff can't help but look at her several more times than he would like to. Luckily, Nichols wasn't aware of most of the glances he stole, at least he doesn't think so. She has yet to say a word, listening and nodding at certain aspects of the story when she hears it for the first time. The undergrowth around the access road has made the hike much more bearable and less strenuous.

They come to a large clearing, where the sawmill once stood. He honestly can't recall the last time he was in this part of the woods. Maybe the trees have enclosed the place further or maybe he is just getting old, but the area looked much bigger to Mitch when he was a kid. They move about the area looking for anything that looks out of place. He is not sure what he expects to find, knowing that any evidence of the sawmill and the fire have long been removed. Nichols has stopped at an area on his left, so he heads over to see what has caught her attention.

Sloane stands solemnly over a small gathering of dead flowers. They aren't the bouquets you might see on the side of the road where a car accident may have taken a life, these are just blossoms from bushes and weeds that grow in the area. They have been piled into a small mound, but they were obviously left here by someone who lost a loved one in the fire. Judging by the wilting and the discoloration, the flowers on the top of the heap have been here for a few weeks. Some of the ones near the bottom of the pile seem to have been left here much longer ago.

While standing next to Sloane, Mitch notices something that he had never seen in any of his trips to the mill before. In front of the pair, on the opposite side of the burn site from the path that led them in, appears to be another path leading away. It is a bit hard to see and camouflaged behind the trees and vines, but there is clearly a path there. Mitch wastes no time in heading in that direction and Nichols follows closely behind.

They fight their way through the shrubs and vines, using their backs to force the branches out of the way. Once on the other side they look ahead at a dirt path, maybe five feet wide. Mitch has been here dozens of times before and has no idea where this path leads. They begin walking, following the bends in the path as it winds back and forth. They stride confidently ahead, while constantly checking their surroundings.

After a severe bend to the right, the path begins to get smaller and leads the officers to a large opening. The trees in this area have all been cleared away, allowing the light from the setting sun to fall heavily on the ground below. On the other side of the clearing, Mitch notices three wooden structures that resemble cabins. He hasn't heard of anyone building cabins in this area, knowing that any local that requested to do so would have been denied by the town administrators.

As they near the huts, it becomes apparent that the buildings are very old and no longer in use. The wood has begun to rot away from the supports, the roofs have openings that no longer protect whatever is inside and the once dark wood has now turned a shade of green due to the presence of moss. When he first laid eyes on the cabins he had hopes that the cabins may be where their suspect had been living. He now knows that there is no way that a person could be hiding out in any of these three buildings, they look like a strong breeze could blow them over at any moment. Sheriff Thompson knows they will need to attempt to get inside the cabins and look around, but he doesn't have much optimism about finding anything worthwhile on the inside.

Just as the sheriff thinks this is going to turn out to be a wild goose chase, the loud voice of Stuart comes over the radio and is noticeably panicked. "Sheriff, I need you to come quick. It's Carter and it's bad. I'm not sure what happened but I think he might be dead."

Mitch takes off in a sprint in the same direction that the pair just came from. When they reach the clearing where the old mill once stood, he stops long enough to ask Stuart over the radio where they are. Stuart replies that he is between the dirt road that leads to the mill from the creek, and the two take off at an even faster pace. Their feet hit hard on the ground, leaving the echoes from their steps to vibrate down the road behind them. This is the first time since entering the woods that

Mitch is not worried about the well-being of Sloane Nichols.

Even though Nichols is in far better shape than Mitch, and runs just about every morning, he has no problem staying ahead of her. His heart is racing and the familiar feeling of having another dead officer is causing his blood to surge through his body at an alarming rate. At random times, Mitch would yell out for Stuart. These woods go on for miles and miles and there is no way to pinpoint the location of the fallen man. Just as Mitch is getting to the point where his feet would not keep going, he hears a faint response from the woods. With a quick glance to Nichols to make sure she has been able to keep up, he leaps through the thick brush on the right side of the road. He uses his forearms to push his way through the vines and branches. He is thankful for his experience growing up in this area, it has taught him how to navigate through the trees with ease.

With a final surge, he stumbles out of the thickness of the pine trees and vines. He practically knocks over Stuart as he emerges, the older deputy doing his best to hold his ground. Deputy Nichols makes her way out of the brush shortly after. There is a small clearing, and Stuart steps to the side revealing a large hole that has been dug in the ground. All three deputies remain silent as they stare down at the body of Deputy Jerome Carter, face down in the hole and most definitely dead.

# *Chapter 15*

The three look down in silence at an eight-foot hole that had been dug out of the dirt. A trip wire must have been used to cause Carter to fall into the hole in the manner he did. When he lost his balance, and toppled into the hole, five wooden stakes were driven through his body and are now sticking out of his back side. One went through his right leg, three though the abdomen and the last one penetrated his face and came out of the back of his head. Each one is stained with blood, the red fluid dripping down the wooden stakes and forming a puddle on the back of the large deputy.

Deputy Carter was slightly over six-feet-tall, and his body is wedged into the hole tightly. His arms are out to his side, resting on the edge of the dirt. Mitch can't begin to imagine what goes through a man's head the moments before he knows he is about to die, but in this case, it had to be nothing more than panic. Mitch climbs into the hole, carefully avoiding the body as best he can. He squeezes his body between Carter and the side walls of the hole and makes his way toward the head of the man. He squats down near his face, which is pointing straight down at the dirt, and can see the eyes of the dead officer. With a gentle stroke, the sheriff closes the eyes and allows the body of Deputy Carter to begin its restful sleep.

Nichols seems to be the one who is the most distressed over what they have seen, for obvious reasons. She was not in town for the incident at Graham Park and judging from her facial expressions, Mitch is guessing she has never seen a dead person before. The fact that they are unable to see the face of Deputy Carter makes it a little easier to deal with. They can look at the body and not see the face of their friend and colleague. Even though he had only been on the force for a brief time, they knew this man. They worked with this man every day.

The officers all begin to meander about and search the surrounding wooded area. Mitch notices that Deputy Nichols is trying to wipe tears from her eyes as she heads to the woods. What is it that makes her so tough; refusing to allow anyone to see weakness in her? Why does she feel the need to compete on such an elevated level with the men that she works with? He stops thinking about her and returns his attention to the area around the body.

Stuart is the first one to call out for the other two. The three again converge on the same location and Stuart points out the tight cable that was tied to two pine trees. It's a simple trip line that has been used in the woods for years. He explains to the sheriff how the two men were making their way toward the mill but had decided to be a few feet apart to cover twice as much ground. Deputy Johnson is visibly shaken by what he found, knowing that it could just as easily have been him that was tripped and ended up in the pit with the wooden stakes.

After some words of encouragement, Mitch convinces Stuart that they need to head back to the other side of the mill and look at the cabins they found. Stuart was a teenager when the fire occurred, meaning he could have knowledge of certain things that the much younger sheriff wouldn't. After hearing Mitch talk about finding the three buildings, Stuart instantly looks off into the distance, trying to find information in his head that had been lost over the years.

"That must have been the buildings where some of the employees lived. There were so many people coming to work at the mill during the busy season that some of them would rent out the cabins and stay there until the season was over. I doubt anyone has been there since the fire."

"I wonder why I never heard anything about people living there," Mitch wonders out loud.

"I'm not surprised, no one wanted to talk about the fire. It was a black mark on the town and most of the people who lived here wanted to put the memories of that day far from their mind, including your father." Stuart has always been careful to speak about the former sheriff with the utmost respect.

"You're probably right. I'm sure nobody has been in the buildings since the fire, they look like they could fall down any minute, but we still need to check them out. Someone is out here doing awful things and we need to find them."

He worries briefly about leaving the body of his fallen officer in the hole but feels confident that it is best if all three of them stay together. The body is lodged in the hole and may take many more hands than they currently have to get the large man off the wooden skewers. He peers at Sloane who has gathered her composure and appears ready to proceed.

The sun has sunk even further behind the trees, meaning the areas that are now shaded by the branches of the tall oaks and pines are becoming increasingly dark. Time is ticking quickly as the three officers make it to the place where the dirt road turns into the clearing that once held the bustling sawmill. Deputy Nichols points out the spot where she found the stash of dead flowers to Stuart, who gives them a once over before catching up to the other two, who have begun forcing their way to the previously undetected second path. Even though the two men in the group have lived in Twisted Timbers for their entire life, neither one of them have ever been down this road.

They walk along the new road, side by side with Sheriff Thompson in the middle of the group. The entire area is almost dark now and the three deputies have each brought out their flashlights. The familiar bend in the road lets Mitch know that they are approaching the shacks that they found earlier. Stuart is the first to reach for his weapon, followed closely by Nichols. Mitch is confident, or naive, enough to continue to proceed without feeling the need to draw his pistol. His father was a big proponent of settling things without the use of a weapon, although Mitch is quite certain his father had never been shot at by a person with a bow.

Once they arrive at the shacks, each deputy takes up a post near the front door of a different structure. Mitch stays outside of the first one, thinking if it's clear he will work his way down the row and can assist Stuart who is waiting to go inside the second building. Nichols has taken up a position near the furthest building and gives a thumbs up that she is ready.

Mitch decides he doesn't want to enter the shack without his weapon after all, the darkness of the area making everything just a bit more ominous and pulls it from the holster. There are no windows in the old wooden building that would give him a hint as to what would be on the inside. He shines his flashlight from side to side as he approaches the front door, which no longer rests in the door frame. As he reaches for the knob, he gives a last look behind him at the other two officers who have their weapons pointed at his building. If there was anything dangerous on the inside, or a person waiting with a weapon of their own, it would take them less than a couple of seconds to come to his rescue. He takes a deep breath and enters the building.

# Kevin M. Moehring

# *Chapter 16*

The door opens easily, almost falling off at the hinges. Mitch enters and shines the light around the room. These buildings were not meant to be luxurious, and the lack of windows points to that fact. The people who slept here would have finished a sixteen-hour shift and only came to these structures to rest long enough to work another long shift the following day. The beam of light reflects off the rusty metal frame of long-forgotten bed frame that is tucked in the corner. He can see the particles of dust that dance in the beam from his flashlight, forced into the air from the sudden emergence of clean air from the outside world. He imagines it has been several years since anyone has entered this building. The air is heavy, and the musty smell makes the sheriff want to cover his mouth.

The shack consists of one medium sized room. Other than the bed in the corner there is no other furniture to be found. There are a few clothes that have been laying on the floor and are now covered in dust following years of inactivity. Mitch continues to look around the room and is relieved to see nothing and, more importantly, nobody hiding in the corners. He returns his pistol to its holster on his hip and his heart begins to slow. He doesn't take time to search every inch of the room, knowing there are two more buildings that need to be cleared.

He steps out of the cabin and back into the fresher Oregon night air. The temperature outside is much cooler than inside the shack. He gives the motion for Stuart to proceed toward the door of his room. He watches intensely as the older deputy walks toward the door, his pants legs still rolled up to his knees. Mitch loses track of the man long enough to steal a look at Nichols, who is the model of professionalism and is adamantly following Johnson with her weapon. The moon is shining through the trees and hitting the side of her face, letting Mitch catch a glimpse of her eyes and how focused she is on covering Stuart. He envies her drive and ambition, both of which can come across as harsh at times.

The deputy enters the second of the three buildings, once again the door swings open as if it would fall off and bang heavily to the ground. The night is silent when you get this far away from civilization. Mitch can hear every breath he takes along with the footsteps from inside the shack. After what seemed like an eternity, Stuart exits the front door and gives each of them an affirmative motion with his right hand. Mitch decides that since nothing was found in the first two rooms that it might be wise for all three to enter the third room together.

He makes his way to Stuart rather quickly and the two men join Nichols near the front door of the third building. He would never tell her that he didn't want her to enter the room by herself because he was beginning to have feelings for her and wanted her to be safe. Instead, he allows her to enter the room first, following at her heels much as she had done to his most of the day. They shine their flashlights in different corners of the room, the added light making it easier to see most of what is inside.

It's obvious that someone has been living in this building. There are two make-shift hammocks that are attached in opposite corners. There are several items of clothing that lay on top of these hammocks, none of which has a hint of dirt on them. The dust and stagnant aroma that filled the first shack, is not nearly as prominent in this room. Mitch looks at Nichols and they both know that things have just gone from bad to worse. Now they are no longer looking for a single person roaming alone in the woods. They are now on the hunt for two people. Two people who have apparently been living in these woods for a while, judging by the worn-out cloth that is used for the hammocks.

Stuart has remained outside while the room was cleared, mostly because the room was too small to hold all three and he feared the structure would collapse under the weight of three adults. The night air is filled with the sounds of the wooden floorboards creaking with every step from the two officers inside. His gun is drawn, and he scans the darkness that surrounds him. He is normally an easy to scare individual, but his senses are on high alert and he is extra jumpy. There are now sounds coming from the woods behind him but being out in the woods at night and after what happened to Carter, he wonders if he is imaging things because his nerves are shot. Branches breaking and leaves rustling cause him to lose focus on the sheriff and Nichols and turn his attention to the trees.

# Evil in the Woods

There is very little light coming down from the moon and his flashlight is failing to brighten the area. It is nearly impossible to make out where one tree ends, and another begins. He calls for Mitch and the sheriff exits the shack in a hurry. Nichols comes out shortly after and stands beside the sheriff, both looking at Stuart with curious eyes. His face is flush red, and his forehead shows the beads of sweat that form when a person is nervous.

"Sheriff, I don't think we are alone. I would almost guarantee there is someone in these woods besides us."

"Why do you say that?" Mitch shines his own flashlight to the trees, but he also finds it difficult to make out features on anything more than ten feet away.

"I'm hearing sounds and we have both lived here long enough to be able to determine which sounds belong to animals and which ones do not."

Mitch trusts that Stuart honestly believes what he is saying. The older deputy has far more experience than Mitch or Nichols when it comes to being in these woods. Mitch knows what the group needs to do next, but he is dreading it with his every fiber. Splitting up has not served him well in the past so he is not looking forward to doing it again. The darkness of the night and the fact that there is a dead deputy not far away makes the decision a necessity.

# *Chapter 17*

The three officers all gather together outside of the middle shack which in turn puts them all right out in the open. There were several minutes of tension as they all brandished their weapons for fear of someone stalking them. They failed to find anyone, and Mitch has begun telling them his plan and why it is important for the group to split up. Someone must stay with the body of Deputy Jerome Carter while the other two return to the police station and get ahold of the coroner from Portland to come and get the body, as well as lobby for reinforcements from the F.B.I. as well as relieve Lucille Pennington who has been manning the office duties alone. Mitch volunteers to be the one to spend the night in the woods and without much disagreement, the other two concede. This is another trait that has been passed down from his father, not allowing anyone else to do the tasks that were the most undesirable.

He reminds them to return at first light and to bring plenty of water as they turn away from him and begin to walk down the dirt road. When they reach the spot where they need to cut through the thick brush to reach the hole that now holds Carter, Mitch is quick to take the lead. He wants the other two to see that he is confident and doesn't fear the upcoming night alone. He can find the pit much easier this second time around, mainly due to the number of branches that have been broken by their first trip. He shines the light down into the hole to make sure that the body was still in place before turning and facing the others.

"You guys get some rest tonight. Stuart, make sure the folks in Portland are aware that the deceased is an officer. If you can, try and get ahold of Agent Walker and ask him to send a couple of agents this way, we may need them."

Stuart nods in agreement and starts to head toward the creek. Nichols begins to follow him but pauses after her first step. She walks slowly over to the sheriff and leans in and puts her arms around his neck. She hugs him tight, but just long enough for her aroma to reach his nose. Even after the exertion of the long hike,

he can still smell the floral scent of her lotion. He thanks
her for her concern and assures her that he will be alright.
He reminds her that he spent many nights in these same
woods when he was a kid.

The two deputies disappear into the trees and
Mitch finds a large tree trunk to sit down beside. He uses
it to hold his back upright and crosses his legs in front of
him. He listens as the footsteps get further and further
away, until he can't hear them anymore. Being alone in
the woods was always a favorite pastime of his, but he
can't remember ever being stuck out here less prepared
than he is right now. He has no water and no food. His
stomach begins to growl which reminds the sheriff that
he was unable to finish his breakfast at the diner earlier
in the morning.

All he has with him is his cell phone, his
flashlight, his police radio and pistol. His body is starting
to send out warning signs that it needs to be rehydrated
after the strenuous activities of the day. He is mentally
strong but that makes no difference when your body is
telling you it needs something. He knows there is nothing
he can do to quench his thirst and tries to put the thought
out of his mind.

He is successfully able to think about something other than food and water. Unfortunately, that something is Sloane Nichols and the hug she gave him before she departed. He still knows very little about her as a person, other than the fact that she longs to compete with the men, she is confident in her abilities and she smells amazing. He sits and ponders the meaning of the hug and if it had the same impact on her as it did on him. He also wonders what the nervousness he feels in his stomach whenever he is around her means. He has often heard people in the movies talk about what it feels like to be in love, but he has no firsthand knowledge of it.

Mitch loses track of his thoughts as he looks up at the night sky. Usually there are thousands of stars that are visible at night. Right now, he is having a tough time seeing more than a couple, mostly due to the cover provided by the numerous trees in the vicinity. He is thankful that since the footsteps of the two officers faded away, the only sound he has heard is that of his own breath and his heart beating. He reaches into his pocket and pulls out his cell phone. He is not surprised to see that he currently has no service. What does worry him is that his battery is not going to last much longer. He decides to switch the phone off, trying to conserve what little bit of life that remains.

Mitch tries to get comfortable on the hard ground. He takes off his long sleeve uniform shirt and rolls it up neatly. He places the rolled-up shirt behind his neck to add some support for his head. He unlaces his boots, just enough so that his feet do not feel so confined. Even though he is stuck in the woods without any of the supplies that he usually takes for granted, Mitch manages to get comfortable enough to nod off.

**Kevin M. Moehring**

# *Chapter 18*

The feeling comes to his muscles sharp at first, like a baseball bat being beaten against his body at a rapid speed. He is awoken so abruptly that it takes him a while to remember where he was when he fell asleep. He is now laying on his back and staring up at the trees as he passes under them. This is not how he expected to wake up. His wrists hurt and his back aches. Every few seconds a new part of his body feels unexpected pain and a new round of agony erupts through his body.

There is no mistaking that his body is moving, even though he is almost certain that his legs are not. He looks over to his right and can make out the face of Officer Carter. The hole from the wooden stake is right in the middle of the man's forehead, splitting his closed eyes perfectly in half. His body is side by side with Mitch's, taking the same bumpy ride. Another searing pain comes from his wrists. They are bound behind his back, making it difficult for him to maneuver in a way that will allow him to figure out what is going on. He is trapped and being drug across the forest floor.

All he can tell is that his feet are also tied together and are elevated higher than the rest of his body. Sometimes when his body goes over a large rock, Mitch can make out a light in front of him. Someone must have come while he was sleeping and tied him up, and they are now dragging him to wherever they want him to go. He can see down to his waist and knows that his service weapon has been removed from the holster. He again wonders to himself how someone could remove his weapon and tie him up without him waking up. He must have been more tired and fatigued than he had originally thought, but then again, he always claimed that he got the best sleep out in the woods.

Yesterday was a very long day that started with a long hike in the woods and ended with him being alone in the forest overnight. No matter how strong a person is, that would wipe out just about anyone. There would surely be ridicule coming his way for having let someone disarm him while he slept, but at the current time, that is not very important to him. If he makes it out of this precarious situation, he will happily take all the ridicule and then some.

The ride continues far longer than Mitch would have liked. Every movement is an agonizing one. He has no idea how long he was asleep or how long this torture has gone on. All that he knows is no matter how hard he tries to break the ropes that hold his wrists, he is unable to create any slack. The movement stops, and for a brief period he can hear voices coming from up ahead. The sounds are not loud enough for him to make out what they are saying, but there are two distinct voices.

His body begins moving again. This time much slower and pulling a little to the left instead of straight ahead. There isn't much light remaining from the fading moon, but what is left gives just enough to allow Mitch to look past the bloody face of Carter and see the same three shacks that they found earlier. He is expecting the trip to end here, but when it doesn't he becomes increasingly panic stricken.

The terrain becomes thicker, heavy bushes and thickets pass under his body with increased regularity. Mitch is trying to keep track of the direction they are heading in relation to the landmarks in the area. It will be easier for him to return to the area if he is able to recall where the location was in relation to the creek or the shacks. His feet become even more elevated above his torso and head, meaning he is being lead up a steep incline.

Another look around, nothing to see other than trees and a dead officer. Suddenly his progress stops abruptly. This time no voices are heard, just footsteps. Someone is heading to where Mitch is tied up and the sheriff is eager to set eyes on whoever is responsible. He lays on his back, his blood pumping in anticipation. He expects to see the person who has been leading him through the woods when his feet suddenly slam to the ground. Just as he tries to raise his upper body to get a peek at what's in front of him, his feet are lifted high once again. Someone obviously cut the rope from whatever it was that was dragging his body and is now pulling him along themselves.

He is being dragged slowly, off to the right, and getting further away from where the body of Deputy Carter remains. He can now see the horse that was being led through the woods with two bodies tied behind it, a large chestnut Arabian that would have no trouble pulling two full grown men. The ground he is being pulled through has gotten much smoother. He can turn his body a little easier now that he is not moving so quickly, even though it hurts to do so.

The view off to his right has changed drastically. Once where the bloody face of Deputy Carter was the only thing he could see, now he can look out thousands of feet and see the Hidden Creek valley far below. They have obviously made their way up the sides of one of the large hills that look down on the creek and the whole town of Twisted Timbers. Another tug on his feet and he is being led further away from the edge. A few more steps and painful tugs of the rope, and a piercing light finally begins to reach his eyes.

The green, lush forest has now given way to brown, rock walls. The flickering light suggests that torches have been stationed along this path and keeps it very well lit. Once again, the movement stops, and he is left to look up at the ceiling, also illuminated by the flames. Mitch is running through the possible places he could be, but in all his years growing up in this area he has never heard of a cave nearby. That doesn't mean that there isn't one, the forest covers thousands of square miles

"This one is awake," comes a deep voice from behind Mitch. He twists his head around trying to see where the voice comes from and is greeted with a powerful stomp to the head. He looks up to the bright ceiling and feels another strong kick to his side. He grimaces in pain and his eyes become watery. The tears clear just before he watches the bare foot come straight down on his forehead. This kick knocks him out.

# *Chapter 19*

The pounding in his head is almost unbearable. He can feel the dried blood that has run down his face and can see it pooling on the dirt below his face. He spits out a stream of saliva that is an alarming shade of red. He is alive and that is the best thing that he could hope for in the current situation. His arms are still tied behind his back, but his legs are now free, allowing him to sit himself up against the rock wall. For the first time since falling asleep against the tree trunk, Mitch can see all his surroundings.

He has been taken to a cave. It's not like some of the caves he has seen in movies or magazines. This one looks to be dug out manually. There are no odd shaped rock formations that protrude from the ceiling or the floor, all the walls and ceiling here are jagged, as opposed to the smoother walls on the caves that are created naturally by water eroding the rocks over time.

He wonders if it would be possible for two people to dig a hole in the side of a mountain as large as this one, and if so how long that would take them.

The part of the cave where he has woken up is not very big at all. If he were to lay down, he would probably touch both side walls with his head and feet. He can see the opening to his room is not as wide as the rest of the cave and the path that leads to where he is extends at least thirty feet. Far in front of him he can make out a large fire at the end. On the other side of the fire is another smaller opening, much like the one that leads to the small area where he is now.

From where he sits there is no sign of the two people who brought him here. He can hear nothing other than the crackling of the fire and the loud thumping that is coming from inside his own head. He uses his back and thighs to push himself up against the rock wall and stand up. The low ceiling of the room makes it impossible to rise completely, so he is left to slouch slightly. Mitch takes a second to look himself over, his work pants are covered in dirt and his white undershirt is no longer the same color as it was when he put it on. He slowly begins to head to the opening that leads out to the rest of the cave structure when he hears feet hitting the hard floor. He leaps back and tries to position his body in the same manner it was when he woke up. This time though, he makes sure his eyes can look out of the opening and down to the fire in front of him.

A person comes walking from the left side of the pathway and heads toward the area where the fire is. On his back, Mitch can see the unmistakable outline of an axe. This must be the same person who left the surprise package on the steps outside of the police station. Mitch watches the man walk away from him, making certain to not make any sounds that would draw the man's attention towards his room. The last thing he wants is for the man to know that he has woken up and suffer another round of blows to the face.

The man turns right before getting to the fire room, disappearing for a moment. When he returns, he is dragging a rope behind him with the body of Deputy Carter attached at the other end. The man pulls the body of the fallen deputy into the furthest room, the one with the fire, and disappears once again behind the rock wall. Mitch can catch glimpses of the man from time to time but is never able to see his face, only his back and the shadows he throws against the opposite wall.

The man bends over, straining to move the large body of the fallen officer into the position he wants it. The black clad man removes the axe from its sling on his back and raises it over his head. Mitch almost gasps loudly as the man swings the axe down in a single violent arch. The light from the fire glistens off the drops of blood that go flying from the blade. The man then moves a little to his right and swings the axe again. The sound of the axe hitting some sort of rock echoes through the confined quarters and gives the sheriff chills up and down his body.

Even with not having eaten in almost an entire day, Mitch finds himself fighting the urge to vomit. The man disappears from his sight but the sounds of the axe contacting the rock is deafening. Mitch can taste the adrenaline as he contemplates the mental state of anyone who would be able to perform such a disgusting act. The man has treated the body of a police officer in a similar fashion as a hunter would a fallen buck.

From where he lays on the ground, Mitch can't see how many smaller rooms make up this cave. There must be more, but it could be a couple or as many as a dozen. The long pathway that leads from his little room to where the man with the axe is dismantling Deputy Carter is long enough that there could be rooms this size stretching the entire length. It is also impossible for Mitch to tell where the other person is, the one he heard having a conversation during the long trip to the cave. An attempt to escape would be futile and probably end in his own death, but it might be the only way out of here.

**Kevin M. Moehring**

# *Chapter 20*

Somewhere deep down in his soul, right next to the part that makes him feel odd whenever Sloane is around, something is telling Mitch that he needs to make a run for it. An equally large part is telling him that if he does, he will end up just like Deputy Carter. There are too many things that Mitch just doesn't know that prevent him from making an intelligent strategy regarding getting out of the cave. He has no idea where the other man is or even if there is only the two that he heard talking. He hopes that there is only two, that would be far easier to work around than if there were several more than that. He would still be severely outmatched, not only in size, but also by ability to navigate the woods and move quickly through the trees.

He also has no idea how big this cave really is or what is the best way to get out. For all he knows, the exit could be located on the other side of the fire room. That would mean he would have to get past at least one of his captors to escape. The thought of having to do that makes the hair on his arms stand on end, much like they did when he decided to climb down from the top of the Ferris Wheel a few months back. He knew where he was heading that time, now he would just be walking out into a cave filled with unknowns.

Once again, he hears the familiar sound of feet hitting the ground and looks back at the room where the fire is. He sees that the man is making his way down the long walkway toward his room. Mitch freezes, making sure to hold his breath and only opening his eyes wide enough so he can see out of the tiny slits in his eyelids. He remembers using the same technique when he was a young boy, trying to appear asleep when his father would come home from work late at night.

He is relieved to see the man's face finally. It's not a face that Mitch remembers ever seeing. The hair on his face is unkempt and tangled in a dark colored beard. His skin is rough and filled with wrinkles, toughened by years spent living in the elements. The size of the man is not imposing but he has a dangerous look about him. Mitch thinks that the man is probably the same height as he is, but the lower body of the hairy man is much thicker. His clothes look to be nothing more than a few pieces of fabric that have been tied together just well enough to prevent them from falling off.

Mitch is intrigued to finally get a view of one of his captors but as the man approaches once again, he begins to fear for his life. He watched as this man carved up his former deputy with just a few blows from his axe. If the man knew Mitch was awake and watching him, the sheriff would surely feel the full wrath of the stranger. The man is only a few feet from the opening to the little room where Mitch is pretending to be asleep when he turns to the right and is no longer in view. Mitch breathes a sigh of relief.

He remains motionless for several minutes, remembering that there were two men who were talking while he was being pulled behind the horse. He begins plotting an escape from this tiny rock room and out of this cave structure, but he does it all while lying motionless on the dirt floor. Several minutes pass without sight of either man, with each second giving Mitch more and more confidence that he is alone in the cave. In his head, he is trying to build enough courage to get himself out of here, knowing that staying put where he is would be the end of his life.

He once again uses the wall to prop himself up, this time remaining seated on his butt with his back against the rocks. He remembers a few years back when he had to arrest a couple of drunk kids after a long night at the Bottom Dollar. When he got the two young men out of his car at the station, they had both managed to get their cuffed hands in front of their body. He was curious about how they had managed to do it, so he asked his father if he knew how it was possible.

Instead of just telling Mitch how the guys did it, his father put Mitch in cuffs and explained to him how to get his hands in front of his body. He is trying to remember every word his father said, now that his hands are behind his back and he needs to be able to use them to get out of here. He places his feet flat on the ground and uses his strong thighs to press his back firmly against the wall. He pushes hard enough to raise his butt far enough off the ground so there is enough space as to allow his hands to slide past.

His first attempt is unsuccessful and quite painful. He moved too quickly and caused his body to land on top of his hands and cause them to twist around in a very uncomfortable way. He manages to refrain from screaming as the pain from his hands reaches the rest of his body and he quickly lifts his rear end up again. This time he remembers to slide his hands down his back side slowly. He feels his biceps burn as he tries to extend them the length needed to achieve his goal. The rope burns into his wrists from the strain of his arms trying to widen as far as possible. Finally, he feels his hands hit the back of his thighs.

It's in times like these that Mitch is thankful that he is still young enough to maneuver his body in the ways needed to finish the rest of the job. He bends his knees and leans into them from the waist. He remembers his father telling him that most people fail at this because they try to move their hands over their feet, and that the trick is to move the legs inside of your hands. Mitch lays his hands on the dirt floor as far in front of his body as he can. He begins with the left leg and manages to tuck it inside of his left arm with relative ease. He follows with the right leg and has no trouble freeing that one either. He pulls his arms up and stretches them above his head to stretch out the muscles and allow the proper blood flow to return. To say that he is impressed with himself would be an understatement.

His next priority is to get the rope off and free his hands completely. He brings his hands near his face, the little bit of light from the torches that reach this room make it hard to see more than a foot in front of him. The rope is made of vines that have been woven together to form cordage. When his hands were behind his back, Mitch would have sworn that a thick rope had been used. He never imagined that weaving a few plants together could produce cordage strong enough to secure his hands so tightly. Now that he is seeing the way the handmade rope has been tied around his wrists, he knows that it will be easier to free his hands than if actual rope had been used.

He studies the knot and the places on his wrist where the vines wrap around. He is trying to follow the process on how the strangers tied his hands together, looking for the one spot that would be the easiest for him to gnaw through. He separates his palms to tighten the vines as tight as possible and finds the spot he determines to be the weakest, right near where his thumb meets the rest of his hand. He digs into the vine with his two front teeth, pulling about half of the width away as far as he could from his hands. He grinds his teeth, trying to saw them through the thick vines. He can hear the fibers breaking almost one by one.

Several more bites and the rope has become about half as thick as it was when Mitch first started his oral assault. He begins to twist his wrists in opposite directions, hoping he is now strong enough to snap the remainder of rope away. When he gets the remaining cordage as tight as he can, he takes a deep breath and yanks his hands apart in a single strong motion. To his relief, his hands break free and fly above his head, his right hand contacting the rock wall and filling the air with a loud thud. Mitch panics and holds his breath, fearing he will soon hear the footsteps coming to his room. The sound never comes.

**Kevin M. Moehring**

# *Chapter 21*

Sound travels easily in a cave. Much to his delight, the thud from his hand banging against the wall has brought no repercussion. Mitch rises to his feet, shaking his legs thoroughly to allow the blood to begin to circulate properly, and makes his way to the edge of the room he has been in. He stops near the opening, listening intently for any sign of movement nearby. He is content that neither of his captors are racing back to find out where the sound came from. He peeks his head around the corner and for the first time he can get a view of the entire cave system where he has been trapped.

He can see that the cave is set up much like a hallway in a hotel. A narrow passage leads from his room to the room at the other end where the fire is still blazing, and the body of Deputy Carter was dismantled. On both sides of the pathway are openings in the wall like the one where Mitch stands. He counts six rooms that come off the main pathway, including the one on the right nearest his room, where the bearded man walked a few moments earlier.

He inches out of his room slowly, trying to remain silent and keep his ears open for any sound that echoes along the corridor that didn't come from him. With his body pressed against the wall, he side-steps his way along the wall until he reaches the opening of the room where the man with the axe exited. He bends his head around the corner and is relieved to see the light from the rising sun sending rays through the opening at the other end. Mitch had planned on it being much harder to find the exit to the cave but is relieved that he will not have to go through the rest of the cave, especially the room with the fire and body parts of Carter. It was bad enough having to look the dead man in the face while they were both being brought here.

The only thing separating Mitch from escaping from this cave and being back in the Oregon forest is about ten feet of cave floor. He checks both sides of the room thoroughly before he makes his way into it. He focuses on his senses, trying to listen for the faintest sound coming from outside the cave opening. He knows that there could be any number of dangers waiting for him outside these cave walls, including the man with the axe, but he has no plans to wait around for them to return. He stops when he gets about halfway to the exit and reaches up to grab a lit torch that was stuck into a crack in the rock wall.

With torch in hand, he takes the first step out of the cave and into freedom. The cool morning air hits his face and the fresh smell of the pines is a welcome change to the mustiness that was inside the cave. He quickly looks around and notices the horse is no longer tied up where it had been left earlier, which he considers to be a good sign. When he was contemplating the best way to get out of the cave, he never gave a moment's thought about what he would do once he got out.

He decides to head in the direction the captors would least expect him to. Mitch moves quickly, making his way further up the hill with every step. Still holding the torch makes the trek even more difficult, but the sheriff has a use for the flame. He continues to jog as fast as he can until he is completely gassed. He hasn't eaten or had any fluids in almost a day and his body is not responding like it normally would. He leans against a tall oak and takes in a long breath of air. After a quick look behind, he is happy that he has made it far enough from the cave that the two abductors would not be able to hear him if he made too much noise.

He stopped in is surrounded by tall trees and fallen branches. He props the torch up against the oak where he was once leaning and begins gathering as many of the dead pieces of wood as his arms would hold. In a small opening between the trees he begins to stack the pieces of wood in a large pile. Next, he finds as many green branches as he can and throws them on top of the dead wood. He needs the moisture inside the newly fallen limbs to produce enough smoke to achieve his goal. He grabs the torch and the pile of wood begins to burn almost instantly. When the wood becomes completely engulfed in flames, he fears that there is not nearly enough smoke. Mitch begins to gather as many fallen leaves as he can possibly find. Usually when starting a fire, he would only look for the leaves that were completely dry. On this occasion, he is looking for exactly the opposite. Leaves that are still wet from the morning dew would burn, but they would also let out a continuous plume of smoke, which is the effect Mitch is hoping for.

# Evil in the Woods

It doesn't take him long before he feels like he has thrown enough wet leaves on the fire to keep the smoke burning for a while. His initial reasoning for creating so much smoke was to signal to Stuart and Nichols where he is, since they expect him to be waiting for them next to the hole that once held Deputy Carter. Now that he is standing here watching the smoke fill the sky, he also realizes that it may give his captors his location as well. In a panic, Mitch begins to look around the area nearest the fire. He needs a tree that is easy to climb but is also high enough to give him an unobstructed view of the fire and area around it.

Every boy that grew up near the Oregon forest has become an expert at climbing trees. Even though it has been several years since he last tried to do it, Mitch has no problem climbing from branch to branch and making his way up the inside of a large pine tree. Once he gets about fifty feet above the ground, he stops climbing and begins to position his body on one of the branches. He is content that this is the safest place to be and the spot allows him to look down and see the fire. He can almost make out the opening of the cave where he was held and further down the hill, the glimmer of sunlight shining off Hidden Creek is faint but recognizable.

Mitch looks up at the blue sky, happy that the smoke trail from the fire he built has done its job. The smoke should be easy to spot from the area where he was supposed to be found by the other deputies this morning. He has no way of knowing how long he will need to be up in this tree and his throat is longing for water. His muscles are burning and trying to cramp up from the energy he has had to use in the last few hours. Stuart will be anxious to come back to the woods and meet the sheriff. Mitch just hopes that comes early enough to get to him before the man with the axe and his partner return and figure out they have lost a prisoner.

He would be trapped in the top of this tree if the captors were to be the first to find him. There wouldn't be much he could do to avoid being captured for a second time, especially if the second man still has his bow. All Mitch can hope for, if they were to come looking for him, would be that they would be unable to find him in the tree and he could remain hidden until reinforcements arrived. That could make for a very long day, and if the smoke died out before Stuart or Nichols knew that it was a signal intended for them, it could lead to even bigger problems.

Kevin M. Moehring

# *Chapter 22*

With sweat dripping down his face, Mitch keeps his gaze affixed on the forest floor. While he was climbing the tree, he had no real intention to get this high off the ground. His resting place is more than fifty feet off the ground, making it nearly impossible for him to hear footsteps if the bad men were heading his way. It would also make it impossible to know if Stuart and Sloane had seen his smoke signal and knew what it meant. Unless they were right underneath him, he would probably not even know they were there.

Mitch is bent at the waist and his calves are starting to burn. A part of him wants to try to sit down on the branch where he is currently standing, but he knows that would make it harder for him to see directly below him. It would also make it more difficult to move and avoid confrontation should the men from the caves find him first. He decides to remain still for the time being. The morning air is still cool on his skin and the silence from being so high has given him enough piece of mind that he can think clearly enough to begin hypothesizing over who the two men could be and what their motives are.

There are literally dozens of scenarios running through his mind about the identity of the men. He didn't recognize the face of the man that he could see while he pretended to be asleep. That negates the fact that the man is a local, Mitch would surely have recognized him if he was. He quickly dismisses the notion that either of the two men are somehow related to the events that happened at Graham Park during the offseason. The feds were thorough in their investigation leaving no stone unturned and little chance that two men would have escaped without anyone knowing they were there.

Mitch can't get past the way the man looked. The shaggy beard, loose fitting clothes that appeared to be sloppily made and the skin on his face looked more like leather. These physical attributes lead Mitch to deduce that the man is some kind of outdoorsman, one of the people like the sheriff has seen on television who choose to live out in the woods and survive on what they can hunt or gather. His father, when he was still alive, would often watch the nature shows that followed people who choose to live off the grid and off the land. This would justify the way the man looked, but it would not explain the horrific acts the man was carrying out.

Mitch thinks back to seeing the body of Deputy Carter for the first time. The wooden stakes exiting the back of the man from his torso and skull. He remembers the piercing sound of the axe contacting the stone, just as clearly as he heard it when he was still in the cave. The sound alone was traumatizing and will probably stay in his mind far longer than he would ever want it to, much like many of the images from Graham Park. He has not told anyone about the nightmares he still has about that night, and now he fears that the things he has seen in these woods will only increase his inability to get a good night's sleep.

Almost losing track of his current predicament, Mitch quickly scans the ground below him for any movement. Another look at the fire and he is happy to see that the pine straw is still smoldering, and the smoke reaches high above where he is sitting. The sun is much higher in the sky now, successfully burning off the remainder of the morning dew from the branches. The firmer footing makes him feel more confident about making his way around to the other side of the tree, opening a new view of the ground below.

It's not long after moving to the opposite side that he sees movement below. He holds his breath, hoping to stay quiet enough to avoid being detected from whoever is lurking below. From where he is perched it is hard to make out someone so far below, but her blonde hair is all he needs to see to know that he is looking down on Deputy Nichols. A powerful sense of relief rushes through his body and he remains frozen for a second. He rarely gets a chance to watch her without her knowledge. He can make out her lines and the tone of her body. She came dressed in similar workout clothes as he saw her in yesterday. The tight leggings crease behind her as she slowly walks around the fire and the loose-fitting tank top allows enough of her black sports bra to show through to peek any man's interest.

He stares so long that he starts to feel guilty about ogling the woman without her knowledge. He knows that he needs to get down to the ground but wants to make sure that his focus is on the descent as opposed to the curves of her body. He waits a minute or two to see if she will walk out of his sight, which she doesn't. He tries yelling for her, but his body fails to release an audible sound. His throat is dry, due to lack of hydration, and it's painful to even get a whisper to exit his mouth. Finally, he decides to break off a smaller branch that is extending from the larger one he has been standing on. He takes aim and tosses it softly toward Nichols. The twig may have been too small, or his aim was atrocious because it begins to flutter off target. It bounces off a lower branch and then another before falling to the ground harmlessly without making a sound.

He has not seen Deputy Johnson yet, but he knows the older deputy is down there somewhere. He loses sight of Deputy Nichols as she walks off to the left, so the sheriff begins to make his way down the inside of the tree, with much more trouble than he did when he climbed up. On the ascent, his adrenaline had been working overtime. That mixed with the strain on his muscles from the squatting on the upper branch to remain hidden has burned through what little bit of energy he had in his thighs. He takes the steps slowly, only lowering himself onto a new branch when he is certain that his hands have a strong hold on the tree to help with his balance. His knees begin to shake uncontrollably.

Another step, followed by another and he is now midway down the tree. He stops to catch his breath and look around once again for his fellow officers. They are nowhere to be seen and he has not laid eyes on them for the entirety of his descent. Mitch thinks about trying to yell out for them again, but he is barely able to swallow and knows any attempt would be futile. He begins to worry that they have moved on and will not be there to assist him when he gets to the bottom. He is now at the point where going back up in the tree is not an option. He has burned through too much of his energy reserve to make it back to where he had been hiding. His choices are to stay where he is or continue to the bottom. The area of the tree where he has stopped is mostly hidden behind the large pines branches, but if the men from the cave were to walk nearby, they would surely see him.

His ability to calmly judge the pros and cons of his precarious situation is disrupted by the sound below him and the vibrations of the tree. Mitch grabs tightly for the trunk of the tree, fearing that he would lose his balance and tumble the remaining thirty feet to the ground. The vibrations shake his body every couple of seconds and each time it causes him to hold on tighter. He can feel the dry bark crumble under the pressure of his hands, which are now covered in sap and refuse to let go of the wood shards that cling to his skin.

Mitch has never been one to talk to himself, but right now he is mumbling to himself quietly. He has no idea what is going on, but he knows it can't be good. He tells himself to calm down and take note of his surroundings, a lesson his father drilled into his head at every opportunity. He checks the fire that he set and even though it is slowly dying down, the trail of smoke is still prevalent in the sky. He follows the path from the fire to where his tree meets the sky, just as another vibration rattles his bones.

**Kevin M. Moehring**

# *Chapter 23*

Mitch is surprised that he was unable to hear the axe striking the tree. He looks down on the man from the cave who had previously used the very same axe to dismember Jerome Carter, now attempting to fell the tree that the sheriff has been using for shelter. Fear races through his body and he can feel his heart practically beating out of his chest. His hands are sweaty causing his grip on the trunk of the tree to be far less stable than he would like it. Mitch steals another glance down at the man just as his weapon makes contact with the tree again.

He starts going through scenarios in his mind on how he is going to get out of this situation. The man with the axe is willing to do anything to get to Mitch, as was proven when he systematically dismembered a police officer hours ago. The sheriff is also aware that Nichols and Johnson are nearby, and surely, they must hear the steel ripping through the tree. He could try to scream out for them, but that could put their lives in further danger. Even if he was able to get a sound to exit his mouth, Mitch does not want to do something that would endanger the safety of the other two officers. The only thing he can see is the top of the stranger's head and the swing of the man's shoulders as his torso pivots every few seconds.

Mitch scurries from branch to branch, trying to get as close to the bottom as he can without the man being able to reach him. The man below him is strong and works the axe in a feverish pitch. Large chunks of the soft wood fly through the air with every strike of the blade. The base of the tree is at least two feet thick but by the looks of things, the man has almost made his way halfway through in just a few minutes. Mitch is thankful that he chose such a thick tree to climb into, wishing that he had decided on this tree because he was smart enough to see what was coming. In no way, could anyone have predicted that he would be trapped in a tree while a madman stood at the bottom, trying to cut the tree down to get to him.

Another few steps down and the sheriff is only about ten feet above the man. The sound of the axe stops momentarily and Mitch freezes in place. He looks under his armpit and watches as the man moves to the other side of the trunk. Like a machine, he begins striking the opposite side with the same fury he showed earlier. Mitch knows he must do something and do it quickly. If he decides to stay put, the man will cut completely through the large tree and be waiting to pull his body out of the fallen timber.

He has nothing on his person that will aide him in his attempt to get out of the tree and avoid the lunatic at the bottom. His firearm and all his belongings had been stripped of him before he had woken up and even his belt was missing from his pants. Luckily, his abductors left the laces in his boots and Mitch eyes the untied strings with curiosity. Would it be possible to somehow use one of the strings to choke the man unconscious from behind, he wonders to himself?

He realizes that he doesn't have a lengthy list of options, reaches down for his boot and begins to remove the laces from the right one. He uses one hand to thread the string through the eyelets one by one, keeping his other hand gripped tightly to the tree. Every few seconds another whack comes from below and the tree shakes violently. He is bent at the waist and in a vulnerable position. It would be far too easy to lose his balance and fall to the ground, surely making his capture easy for the man with the axe.

Once he has the string free from his boot, he wraps the end around his palm with a few twists. The rope is far shorter than he expected it to be and Mitch is concerned that there will not be enough room left once he wraps the other end around his other hand. He decides he will need both laces and will simply tie them in a knot, making the two laces a single, longer string. This will allow him to wrap the ends around his hands more times and still have enough room to gather the middle of the rope around the man's neck and hopefully suffocate him from behind.

After successfully removing the second string, leaving the tops of his boots open and loose, Mitch is happy with the length of the rope. He now has them securely wrapped around his hands and there is still plenty of room in the middle to get around the neck of the man with the axe. A few strong tugs with his hands and the knot seems to be holding tight. He unwraps his left hand, allowing him to use it to hold on to the trunk of the tree as he attempts to get into a better position. He looks down at the man, who has yet to look up at Mitch a single time since he started hacking away at the tree. There is a larger branch directly over where the man is standing but it is a few feet higher up. This would mean the jump Mitch needed to make would be at least fifteen feet to the ground and he would have to land softly enough to be able to lunge for his attacker and quickly get the rope around his neck before the man could react.

The branch that currently holds the sheriff is slightly off to the side of the man below. If he were to drop down from here, he would surely land right in front of the man, making it impossible to secure the rope around his neck without a scuffle. Despite his concerns about the fall, Mitch begins to move back up to the higher branch. He feels the only way for his plan to work is if he has the element of surprise working in his favor. That element would surely disappear if he were to drop down in front of the man.

He can feel his thighs ache as he pushes himself up onto the higher branch. The wood separates at the trunk and divides into two thick branches, both look sturdy enough to hold the weight of the sheriff. He looks down again and heads out onto the bigger of the two branches. He drops himself down to a sitting position, with his feet dangling in the air as if he was a small boy playing in his backyard. His eyes remain focused on the man below, who remains focused on getting the tree down. He again wraps the string around each of his palms, pulling them tight to make sure he will have the required leverage. With a small scoot of his rear end he is heading for the ground. From a place inside that he tries to keep hidden, a deep roar comes from his gut and echoes through the woods as his feet hit the dirt below.

## *Chapter 24*

Tumbling to the ground and coming to a rest on his backside is not something that Mitch had planned on. He may have misjudged the distance he had to fall, and his body began travelling faster than he had anticipated. Regardless, he can leap to his feet and get behind the man while the burly guy was in the middle of a swing of the axe. With a surge of adrenaline Mitch throws his hands over the guy's head and pulls tightly on the string. For a moment, the man doesn't move at all. Sheriff Thompson crosses his right hand over his left trying to put more pressure on the string and cut off the man's air flow.

The man drops the axe and uses both hands to tug at the piece of string around his neck. Faint groans can be heard coming from his mouth as he is gasping for air. Mitch raises his right leg and places his knee in the middle of the man's back, creating even more tension on the string and a tighter noose around the neck. Suddenly

Mitch is falling backwards away from the man. He lands firmly on the ground staring up at the tree where he had been hiding moments earlier. His hands are now far apart, the tension on the string finally caused the rope to snap and free the man from the sheriff's grasp. Mitch uses his hands and feet to scoot his body away from the man as quickly as he could. He watches as the man bends over for the axe and begins walking toward him.

Mitch begins asking the man for mercy, saying anything he thinks will make the man reconsider what he is about to do. The look in the man's eyes is pure evil, cold and unforgiving. His face is dirty, and his beard is far overgrown. In the warm summer air, the man is covered from head to toe in thick cloth, mostly black in color, but even with the exertion of trying to cut down a tree, the man looks like he has not even begun to sweat. It's not uncommon to see men on hunting trips cover their skin completely to try to stay hidden, but this man looks to be dressed this way out of lack of options rather than trying to keep the mosquitos from biting. His hair is long, to match his beard, and is thick and greasy. If he had to guess, Mitch would assume this man had been in these woods for a long time.

# Evil in the Woods

The lack of expression on the man's face is what has Mitch worried the most. He is not racing after the sheriff but is walking methodically toward him, stalking his prey with every step. Mitch looks him in the eyes and can see the man has bad intentions. Even though he has little experience dealing with murderers, Mitch knows that the eyes he is looking into right now show little signs of remorse or pity. The crazed man walks forward with his right arm hung low, dragging the axe behind him as he creeps closer. His other hand is rubbing his neck trying to ease the pain from the rope. Mitch thinks about trying to make a run for it but remembers how swiftly the man moved when they were back by Hidden Creek. There is no chance that he has enough energy to outrun someone who moves like that and making this guy mad is the last thing Mitch wants to do.

The man continues to walk down his prey, the sheriff, until there is nowhere left for him to go. Mitch has backed himself up against the trunk of a tall cedar tree, about ten feet away from the fire that he'd hoped would signal to his rescuers. It worked like it was supposed to and the rescuers came, unfortunately they left before they found him. Now he is face to face with one of the men who kidnapped him while he was asleep and took him to the cave. He utters more words that fall on deaf ears, the man not even beginning to slow his approach. He raises the axe far above his head, never taking his eyes off the sheriff. As the man gets ready to swing the axe down and do bodily harm, Mitch notices a slight smile coming from his mouth, showing off the rotted teeth of the maniac.

The man is standing over him, like a lion who has just caught a gazelle and is making sure there are no other predators around before partaking in the feast. He begins to swing the axe down toward the midsection of the sheriff, aiming for the area just under the breast plate. Mitch reacts instinctively and raises his right leg and with all the energy he has left he kicks the man's knee. The man standing over him is thickly built, with legs not much different than the trunks of the trees that surround them. The kick may not have done much to injure the bigger man, but it had the desired effect in that it caused the first strike to miss it's intended target. The sharp edge of the axe falling painlessly to the dirt on the side of Mitch's body.

The face of the man is now so close to the sheriff that Mitch can smell the man's breath, a putrid aroma.

Mitch grabs him by the side of the head, one of his hands covering each of his ears. Mitch holds him firmly and raises the right leg again and lands a strong kick to the man's crotch. Another lesson Mitch learned in high school, it doesn't matter how big a person is, if you hit them in the right spot, they will feel it. The man groans again loudly, his baritone sounds echoing through the trees. The man takes a few steps back, allowing Mitch to get to his feet and have a fighting chance in the battle.

The two men square off like gladiators in an arena. Mitch is at a distinct disadvantage without any sort of weapon while the stranger is swinging an axe around like it's a toy. They circle each other, one man trying to get closer while the other is trying to keep the distance between them. Mitch can taste the adrenaline pumping through his veins, he can feel his pulse beating in his neck. His eyes remain focused on the man in front of him, ready to make an evasive maneuver in case the man begins to lunge for him. Again, he sees the man curl his mouth in an odd kind of smile just before raising the wooden handle and pointing the sharpened edge of the axe at the sheriff.

He dodges the axe with a quick step to the side and starts to spin back to face the man again. His progress is halted when he realizes that while he was able to avoid the axe, he was unable to get away from the strong left hand of the bearded man. He has grabbed ahold of Mitch's wrist and is squeezing tightly, not allowing the sheriff to escape his grasp. The man pulls hard and extends his thick foot enough to cause the sheriff to trip and fall to the ground.

Once again Mitch is looking up at the man with fear in his eyes, praying for a miracle. This time the man remains at Mitch's side and places his foot on the fallen man's chest. He uses his weight to hold down the sheriff and again raises the axe, this time taking aim at the neck area. Mitch knows that this man is lethal and has no problem cutting a person apart, but this ordeal has gone on far too long and he has used up every ounce of energy his body has to offer. He lays defeated underneath the mystery man, accepting of his fate. He closes his eyes and waits for the surge of pain or the bright light or whatever it is he is expected to feel or see when he dies. Mitch holds his breath and waits for the deadly blow to come.

# *Chapter 25*

After a few tense moments, he has yet to feel the axe drive through his body. Instead he hears the unmistakable sound of a gunshot and the same grunt from the dirty man as he heard when he was trying to choke him with his shoestring. Mitch opens his eyes and the man is trying to limp away from the sheriff, hardly able to put any weight on his right leg. Mitch hears the voice of Sloane Nichols come from behind him and he quickly sits up with renewed energy. The female officer walks right past Mitch as if she didn't know he was there and races around to the front side of the now injured man.

He finds himself watching her far longer than he should instead of getting up to assist her. As he starts to move, another hand grabs his shoulder and pushes him back down to the ground.

"Stay there Sheriff, we need to make sure you're ok." Stuart is dressed in full police uniform and is standing over Mitch.

"Stuart, you guys have impeccable timing. I'm fine, just a little worn out and thirsty." Mitch reaches for a bottle of water that his fellow deputy has carried through the woods. He makes a gesture toward Nichols and Stuart heads off in that direction to assist her. Mitch watches as the man who had the axe is hardly able to keep himself upright and moving.

He downs the bottle of water without stopping for breath, crumbling the bottle and discarding it. He makes his way to his feet and begins the walk forward to where the others are. The man has now fallen to the ground and the two deputies are still struggling to get the man into handcuffs. Mitch quickens his pace a bit but by the time he gets to where they are, the scuffle is over. The once intimidating man with an axe is now laying on his back with blood flowing from his knee. He looks up at them, at no one in particular, his eyes are glazed over, and his stare is terrifying. He has the look of a man who has been in a fight for years and has finally given up all hope of winning.

"Mitch, can I speak to you over there for a minute?" It's on a rare occasion that Stuart would ever call him Mitch, he is a stickler for the rules and calling the Sheriff by anything other than that must mean he has something important to say.

Mitch follows the older officer over to where the fire has all but died out. From behind Mitch can make out that Stuart is not as put together as he is on other days when he shows up for work. The creases that are normally crisp in his slacks are not present and the back of his shirt is showing perspiration stains near the armpits, which seems unusual in the crispness of the morning air. Stuart stops and faces him before beginning to talk in a quiet tone.

"Mitch, I went back to the station last night to do some research. I was around when the fire at the mill happened, and I heard all the rumors, but I didn't really believe any of them. I went digging in the attic, where the files are kept from years ago." Stuart stops long enough to pull a couple of photographs from his chest pocket. "Per the police report, there were two boys who lived in the cabins with their father. After the fire, no one could remember seeing the boys or what happened to them."

Mitch looks at the photos as Stuart holds them in front of his face. The images are old and faded, each picture showing a young boy in jean shorts and no shirt. The boys had long hair and wry smiles on their faces. There is something else in the picture that draws Mitch's attention. In the background of the picture of the older boy is the same cabin that he searched the day before. When you live in an area that uses lumber for every resource possible, you become accustomed to noticing distinguishing features in the wood. That is one of the cabins near the mill.

"At least that explains your appearance today. So, this report you found, do you know who wrote it?" Mitch is still skeptical, thinking that if two young boys had disappeared from the fire that he would have heard about it over the years.

"I was going to bring it with me but as you can imagine it wasn't in the best condition. Your father was the only name on the report, and it definitely looked like his handwriting to me." Stuart is rubbing at his face as he talks, this being the first time he has ever been seen in public with any sign of a five o'clock shadow is starting to bug him.

"Well if it was my father who wrote the report, then there is definitely merit to it. Were the names of the boys listed? Do we know who they are?" He is focused on the faces of the boys in the pictures, but the man they have in custody is far older and covered in dirt and hair. Even if he were a well-seasoned officer, which he of course is not, it would be hard to determine if the man in cuffs is either of these two boys for certain.

"Their father worked at the mill, a man by the name of Benny Hopkins. According to the repot, his wife died when the kids were young, and Benny brought the two boys to the mill with him during the season. The boys go by the name of Butch and Junior Hopkins, once again, per the report." Stuart feels confident that Mitch has seen enough of the pictures and shoves them back in his pocket.

"I still find it hard to believe that after the fire was over, my father didn't think to look for the two boys." His reluctance to believe his father would have made an error so drastic causes Stuart to provide more information.

"It stated in the report that many sources indicated that the boys had not been at the camp when the fire started. I don't know how true that statement is, but that could be the reason that no search was ever conducted. There would have been several people at the site, and they would have been there for several days after the fire. You would think that if there were two young boys in the woods that they would have approached the firemen or investigators at some point."

Mitch is still not buying the story. "OK, let's say for the sake of an argument that these boys disappeared out here in these woods. The fire was almost twenty years ago, do you think it is possible that they have survived out here that long without ever being spotted?"

Stuart has the look of a man who had an exceptional story to tell and someone finished it for him before he could get to the best part. "Maybe not. I just did the research and I'm telling you what I found."

"Stuart, I'm not saying you are wrong. It's just that I find it hard to believe. Does that man look like either of those boys to you?"

"Not really, but it has been almost twenty years and who knows how the elements would change a person's appearance over that length of a time," Stuart says in a matter of fact tone.

Mitch shakes his head slowly, unable to comprehend what Stuart is trying to convince him of. "Did you get any more information on the two hands that were dropped off to us?"

Stuart perks up, "Yes, the feds left me several messages. They are sending some folks this way at some point today. Agent Walker said he had one of his guys do some digging around and it seems that they have a name for the missing female, Erin Winkler. Appears she had been dating Robert Eldrgidge for some time and they were beginning to get serious." He fumbles through a few pages in his notebook. "The feds checked with her employer and she has been on vacation for the last few days and there was no answer at her residence."

"Thanks Stuart, let's go give Nichols a hand and head back to the cave to look around. We are going to have to look for the other man that's out here, the one that likes to use the bow and arrow."

# Kevin M. Moehring

## *Chapter 26*

Maybe Stuart was unaware that there was a second man that they needed to find, which wouldn't be too much of a stretch since Mitch is the only one to have witnessed the two men at the same time. Deputy Johnson had been mumbling under his breath the whole time they made the short walk over to where Sloane has been standing next to the cuffed stranger. The man lays motionless, still with the eerie look in his eyes as he stares off into the distance as if judging the meaning of life.

Mitch takes this time to tell the two deputies about his adventures in the early morning hours. How he woke up being dragged through the forest and ending up in the small room in the cave. He left out several details about the butchering of Carter, deciding to simply tell them that their former friend had been mutilated. He also omits several details about how he was able to escape the cave and make it to the tree, opting to give them the shortened version to speed things along.

"Stuart tells me we have a name for the missing girl, I guess the next thing we need to do is find her. I say we start in the cave, there were several little coves built into it and I didn't take the time to check them out before I got out of there."

Nichols nods in agreement and gets assistance from Stuart in picking up the man. They each stand on opposite sides of him with one arm wrapped around his, in the small opening between the elbow and his ribcage. Mitch leads the way to the cave with his head on a swivel. He knows there is another man out here somewhere and it will only be a matter of time before the man shows up looking for his partner. It has also occurred to the sheriff that the man could be hiding in the cave waiting on them to enter before attacking them. Another possibility that Mitch has pondered is that the man is stalking them; staying out of sight but following their every movement and waiting for the perfect opportunity to take them out.

Mitch stops abruptly and turns to Stuart, "Did you happen to bring an extra gun with you?"

"No, I didn't. We didn't know that anything had happened to you, so we didn't think we would need any extra fire power. I do have my Taser though, you are welcome to it."

Mitch grabs the Taser and holds it in his hands like it was a real gun. It's much lighter and doesn't do nearly the same amount of damage, but for once he is thankful for his friends at the F.B.I. They used some of the recovered funds from the Graham Park case to send several items that they felt every respectable police department should have, including the Tasers.

Feeling slightly more confident, Mitch begins to make his way down the hill toward the cave. He is trying not to let on that he has no idea where he is going. When he left the cave, he didn't bother to pay attention to which way he was heading. His only intention was to get as far away as possible and get to higher ground to make it easier to signal for help. The coolness of the morning air has dissipated, and the late morning humidity is making the trek harder as Mitch is once again parched and wishing he hadn't finished the entire bottle of water in a single drink.

He remembers seeing the fallen oak tree that he steps over painfully. He waits to assist the other two in making sure the prisoner cooperates and clears the tree. For some reason, Mitch is drawn to the man's feet. He is barefoot, walking over sticks, branches and rocks with ease, and showing no signs of discomfort. As the man swings his foot over the branch, exposing the bottoms of his feet, Mitch can see that the skin on his soles is thick and tough like leather. He wonders to himself how long this man has been going around barefoot in the woods.

They continue walking down the side of the hill in silence, except for the random four-letter word that would come from Stuart every time he nearly tripped. The sheriff leads the group slightly to his right, where he can see the stump that had held the horse when he was brought into the cave. He is lucky to have found the same spot again, and glad that he wouldn't be embarrassed in front of the other deputies if he had led them in the wrong direction all this time.

He stops short of the cave and ponders if he should fill in the other two on just how badly Carter's body had been treated. It wouldn't be right for them to walk into the cave and stumble on the dismantled body of their former colleague. He struggles to find the words to express the vulgar nature with which the man in cuffs treated their friend, but Mitch finds a way to get the sentiment across. He wants them to know just how dangerous the man they have in custody can be. How easily the man they are holding butchered up their friend as if he was just a piece of meat.

Before Mitch starts to turn and enter the cave, he shares a look with the prisoner once more and notices the same evil grin across his face. Not only was the man cold-hearted enough to cut up a human being, now he is crazed enough to smile when hearing the gory details. Mitch has had enough of the crazed man and reaches over and gives him a strong whack in the face with his right hand. He can't remember the last time he punched someone, but this seemed about as good of a time as any to break the streak.

Deputy Nichols looks unaffected by the details she has just heard. She stands firmly, holding on to the arm of the man, with little to no expression on her face. Mitch settles on the fact that she is once again trying to impress the men around her and not wanting her emotions to be exposed. Even the toughest of men would have some sort of facial gesture once they hear of how their friend had been treated after he was dead.

The group takes the last few steps to the front of the cave. Sheriff Thompson peers inside and can see all the way back to the room that had the large fire and now also holds the pieces of Deputy Carter. He is relieved to see the fire still burning, since he doesn't have his flashlight. He does find it odd that the blaze is still going but his brain is not functioning at full capacity, so he chalks it up to the cave sheltering the fire from the outside elements. He leads the way into the cave, with the Taser pointed straight out in front of him as if it was an actual gun. The air is heavy on the inside, and the only sounds that can be heard are the crackling of the fire and a few drops of water that are leaking down from the top of the cave.

He heads down the main hallway of the cave. The thick moist air is only covered up by the smell of the fire burning at the end of the walkway. He notices that all the other smaller rooms on either side are far too dark to be able to see inside of without additional light. Mitch heads straight for the room with the large fire in hopes of finding a torch that he can use to search the extra rooms.

He knows that he is going to see far more than he wants to when he enters the room, but he is the sheriff and the other two deputies are looking to him to lead the way. His father would not have thought twice about charging into the room to get what he needed.

With a long deep breath, Mitch gathers enough strength to enter the room at the end of the cave. Luckily, he will not need to use the Taser as the only body he finds inside the small room is in several different pieces and is scattered about the ground. The rust colored fluid that surrounds the pieces of flesh has mixed with the dirt from the ground and created small spots of thick mud. The heat from the fire and the denseness of the air in the small space has caused the body parts to deteriorate faster than they would normally, adding to the pungent odor that monopolizes their senses. Mitch remembers something else his father would tell him. "Once you have smelled a decaying body, you will never forget that smell."

**Kevin M. Moehring**

## *Chapter 27*

Sheriff Thompson spends the next few moments picking up most of his belongings and attaching his work belt. He has only been a police officer for a couple of years, but he has already begun to feel naked without the added weight of his weapon on his hip. He is still missing several items, most importantly the keys to his truck, but he knows there is a spare set back at his office, so he doesn't bother to continue looking for them. Mitch is relieved to see that his flashlight was still operational, meaning the search of the other rooms would be easier. He gives Nichols the Taser and she sticks it into the waistband of her tight pants, covering it with the back of her tank top. The heat in this room is tremendous. The flames reach several feet high above the ground, an impressive feat considering that there has been no one in the room to stoke the fire for some time, at least not that they are aware of.

All three of the officers are facing in the same direction, fearful of what is on the other side of the room. They are all obviously aware as to what is on the other side of the room, but they are not strong enough to look at it any longer than necessary. The warmth of the room has sped up the process and the smell is putrid causing Stuart to hold his hand over his nose. He tries to do it in the most respectful manner, but in typical Stuart fashion, the gesture comes off as childish.

Mitch is the first to look back toward the body. He needs to make sure that there is nothing else in the room that may be of importance. He turns from side to side and other than the fire and the remains of Deputy Carter, the room is nothing but dirt and rocks, including a larger boulder that was once used as a cutting board. He explains to Nichols that she needs to stay put in this room with the prisoner, while they search the other rooms in the cave. She rolls her eyes, obviously disappointed that she has been given the task of being an armed babysitter. Mitch gives her a look to let her know that he is still the sheriff and what he is asking her to do should be considered a direct order. She begins to protest, thinks better of it and nods in agreeance.

Sheriff Thompson walks over toward the man and reminiscent of a move his father would make, delivers a strong kick to the outside of the man's knee, near where the bullet went into his leg not long ago. The strike buckles the burly prisoner and he drops to the ground. A soft moan escapes his lips before he raises his head and looks up at the Sheriff. As if to say he welcomed the pain, the man gives Mitch a sly grin and a wink with his right eye. With a strong whack from the handle of his weapon, Mitch delivers the message to the stranger that he is not intimidated.

"If he moves, empty your clip into him. We'll sort it out later," Mitch tells Sloane.

"Yes sir, Sheriff." Now it appears that Nichols is the one who is giving off a wry smile, happy to be given the green light to shoot the man if he tries to escape.

Stuart follows the sheriff out of the fire room as he begins down the center walkway. Mitch gives the motion that he is going to check the rooms on the right-hand side, and ducks into the first room. Stuart is left speechless in the middle of the cave. He was under the impression that the two men were going to search the rooms together. Even though he would never admit it,

Stuart still has nightmares about the time he spent alone during the Graham Park incident. Now he is asked to run into dark rooms in a cave without the help of another officer. For the second time this year he is seriously regretting his decision to be a cop.

He gathers his strength and like a good police officer, enters the first room on the opposite side of the cave. His flashlight moves much faster than he wants it to, but he tries to see as much of the dark room as he can. If something or someone is hiding inside, Stuart hopes that the bright light will stun the person long enough to get a shot off. He practically jumps around the small room. His nerves are rattled, and his adrenaline is pumping. He is relieved to see that this room contains nothing more than wooden crates and boxes. He doesn't take the time to check them to see what is on the inside, quickly backing his way out of the room, relieved to have not found anyone on the inside waiting for him.

Once he is back in the center walkway, Stuart begins to calm down. The light from the fire room trickles down the corridor, making it far easier to see. Stuart sees the beam of light from the sheriff's flashlight peek out from the second room. He races ahead and dives into the second room on his side of the hall. This is not a time for him to be cowardly in the face of danger. He already has a reputation around town of being afraid and he doesn't want Mitch to form the same ideas.

Once inside the small room, Stuart shines his light around again. This time he is much more meticulous and makes sure to hit every corner of the room. His feet are still moving wildly but he has avoided making the small jumps like he did in the first room. In the far corner from the entrance, Stuart sees something that makes him steady his light on it. He walks in a straight line toward it, gun pointed and finger on the trigger. He expects a quick attack from whatever it is. Instead, the thing lays motionless. As he gets closer he can see that it is some sort of handmade blanket fashioned out of large leaves and vines.

He uses his right foot to kick at the outside of the blanket and retreats as if his foot would be grabbed. When nothing happens, he moves in again and gives the heap another kick. Again, no response. Stuart then kneels alongside the pile of leaves and uses the end of his flashlight to remove a sizable portion. Underneath is the body of a woman. Her face is bloody, which matches the rest of her body, and her skin is a pale gray color. He removes the large vines and uncovers her completely. He shouts out for the sheriff who comes running into the room without hesitation.

The two men stand over the body and say nothing. They do not need to be told that this is the missing hiker, Erin Winkler. The lack of a left hand gives them that information. Mitch leans in and shines his light closely on her arm, concentrating on the area where her hand used to be. It has been burned severely, the blood has hardened and stains what remains of her arm in a copper tone. From his crouch, he looks up to Stuart to make sure he understands what happened to the lady's hand. Mitch sticks two fingers on the woman's neck, checking for a pulse. He stops for a moment and puts his ear next to her mouth, then returns his fingers to her neck.

"She's still alive. I found a pulse, a faint one, but I still found a pulse. Let's hope those boys from Portland get here soon." He stands back up next to Stuart.

"I understand seeing all of the blood around her waist and her arm, but why is there so much on her face? I'm sure when they cut her hand off, she held it against her body. That explains all the blood on her lower half. I just can't come up with a good explanation as to why her face is covered in blood." Stuart is always the logical one, pointing the obvious flaws in a story, sometimes even before he knows all the information.

"When I was checking for a pulse, I noticed she no longer has a tongue. You can't tell from where you're standing, but it's missing. I'm guessing she was in severe pain once they cut her hand off and even more when they stuck it in the fire to cauterize it. The assholes probably got tired of her yelling in agony that they cut her tongue out." Mitch states the facts in a stern voice, trying not to let Stuart see that he is shaken. "Did you find anything in the first room?"

Stuart doesn't respond right away, left contemplating what it must feel like to have your hand severed, then stuck in a fire and finally have your tongue ripped out. "The only thing in there was some wooden crates. I didn't check the contents." His body is trembling, much as you would expect a small boy to do when he thinks he has just seen a ghost.

"It's not important. I checked all three of my rooms. Nothing much in there but some old bones, tools and pieces of rope. I'll go check in the last room and you stay here with her. I know it doesn't look like it, but she can hear you. Talk to her, tell her everything is going to be alright." Mitch is trying to stay calm while giving Stuart optimism regarding the condition of the woman. In reality, Mitch knows that there is very little chance she will survive. She has lost a lot of blood and has gone through severe trauma, and it's only a matter of time until her body gives in to the pain.

Stuart says nothing. Just kneels alongside the body of Erin Winkler and stares at her. Before Mitch leaves the room, he looks back again. Stuart has still not uttered a word but has made it as far as tapping on her head as if he is afraid to touch her. The sheriff doesn't know if Stuart is capable of relaying the feeling of comfort to anyone, but he knows that the deputy would risk his life to protect the injured woman if all hell broke loose before the Feds arrived, and that's the kind of officer Mitch is happy to have on his side.

Mitch heads to the last room in the hallway. He walks inside without fear, shines his light around and is met with a wall full of newspaper articles. He walks closer, shining his light from top to bottom. The entire wall is covered in news print. The paper is very old, some of them are ripped and torn in areas, while others remain fully intact. He focuses his attention on a large section in the middle where the articles appear to be in the best condition. There are clippings from several newspapers, all pertaining to the fire at the saw mill. The various headlines mention the names of the men who died, talk about how the town was ill-equipped to handle such an accident or the lack of a rescue attempt once the police force was on scene. Mitch has heard these stories before, but the fact that these papers are hanging on the wall in this cave might give some prudence to the theory that Stuart came up with last night. As hard as it is for Mitch to believe, these two men could have been the forgotten children of one of the deceased. There is no other explanation for this shrine to be in such an unlikely place.

Mitch knows that Stuart will be glad that his diligence paid off, but Mitch decides to keep the contents of this room private for the time being. He has yet to form a plan that will solidify his theory but when he does, he will need it to be a complete surprise to everyone involved, especially Stuart. He exits the room after being certain that there isn't anything else in there that he needs to be concerned about. When he gets into the hallway he can see the shadow of Sloane in the far room. She is standing fast with her gun drawn on the cuffed man. Mitch thinks to himself how much she is probably enjoying the fact that she has complete control over the prisoner, with a green light to fire at will.

He enters the room where Stuart found Erin Winkler. The deputy is still knelt down beside her, softly removing the hair from her eyes. There is no way to know if the older deputy spoke to the woman while he was out of the room, but Mitch doesn't hear the man say anything to her as he enters. Deputy Johnson jumps slightly when he realizes Mitch is standing behind him and quickly rises to his feet. Stuart uses the palm of his hand to wipe away the last remnants of a few tears before looking the sheriff in the face. "Did you find anything in there?"

"Nothing really. I know you're not going to like this, but you know as well as I do that there is another one of these maniacs running around these woods. We are police officers and it's our job to find him." The sheriff has not lost sight of the main objective, capture both men in the woods and make it out of here alive.

"Sheriff, if we go by the theory that these are the boys from the saw mill, then we have to believe that they are far better suited in these woods than we are. I think it might be best to hole-up here and wait for Agent Walker and his guys to get here." Stuart is not the bravest of men to begin with, he has no problem letting Mitch know that he is not keen on chasing another man around the woods.

"Do you remember what happened when they showed up to Graham Park? Do you remember the way they treated us and how they wanted all the credit? They had no problem throwing you in jail for crying out loud. That is not going to happen this time. This is our town and we are going to handle it." Even though he is fearful of what is in store for them, Mitch has enough bravado to want to handle the job on their own.

The two men make their way back to the room where Nichols has her gun trained on the prisoner, who looks like he hasn't moved a single muscle in the time they were gone. Mitch calmly explains to the female deputy what they found in the other rooms and instructs Stuart to go to the first room on the right and grab some rope. After hearing the condition of the woman, Sloane Nichols shows the slightest signs of rage. Mitch is afraid that she will snap and take her frustrations out on the man in handcuffs. He walks over to her and puts his hand on her shoulder, reminding her that the woman is still alive and will probably make it out of the cave and survive. This is a lie of course, but right now he just wants to diffuse the situation. He also explains to Nichols that she will need to keep an eye on the woman as well as the prisoner while he and Stuart look for the other man in the woods.

"What! No way!" Her voice has risen several octaves, and this is the first sign of emotion that she has showed during the whole ordeal. "First you tell me to play babysitter to this vagrant, now you want me to not only keep an eye on him, but make sure that a woman on her last breath stays alive? I want to be out in the woods looking for the other man. I am more than capable." Her voice has risen several decibel levels and her normally calm demeanor has turned into something that resembles that of a caged animal.

Mitch doesn't quite understand the frustration she is showing. Most people would be happy to stay put in the safety of the cave with a gun pointed on a cuffed suspect. Nichols, however, has the need to be right in the middle of things, to prove her worth whenever she has the opportunity. Her need to impress the people around her must come from somewhere in her past, somewhere Mitch has never visited with her. He makes a note to find out more about the woman once they all make it out alive. Luckily, Stuart rushes back into the room with a bundle of rope slung over his shoulder and breaks the tension.

Mitch takes it upon himself to tie the suspect up with the rope. It's not that he doesn't trust anyone else to do it, it's just that if the man was to escape, Mitch wants to be the one who is to blame. He forces the man's face into the dirt, kneeling on his back for extra leverage. He wraps the rope in a loop around the bare ankles of the prisoner. He pulls the rope tight and wraps the other end around the handcuffs. This forces the man's feet to be up in the air, in the uncomfortable position of being close to his back. He has seen this technique in some of the old westerns his father would watch but has never had to use it until now.

Satisfied with his effort, Mitch stands up and admires his work. For once he is happy for all the times his father forced him to practice tying knots on camping trips. Without looking at Nichols, Sheriff Thompson gives a nod to Stuart to let him know that it's time to go looking for the other man. He catches the eyes of the older deputy who gives an apologetic look to the female officer, saying this wasn't his idea, as if that would things any better. Sloane is upset and feels like she is being left out of the action, which goes against everything she fights for daily. There is nothing anyone can say to her that would make her feel differently. Mitch knows this and heads for the exit of the cave without saying another word. Stuart follows closely behind.

## *Chapter 28*

Now that she is left alone in the cave, Sloane Nichols decides to take some of her frustration out on the man at her feet. She tucks her weapon into her waistband and proceeds to unload with heavy stomps to the man's back. He groans a little and this just infuriates her more. She continues her assault on the defenseless man, as if he is the one who made the decision that she had to stay in the cave and babysit. Stomps and kicks come rapidly, too fast in fact, and she loses her balance and falls to the ground. Her body lands inches from the severed head of Jerome Carter.

She knew the pieces of him were scattered around this room, but she had been able to put it out of her mind up until now. She is so close that she can smell the blood that has puddled under his head. She is relieved that his face is aimed at the wall, so she didn't have to look him in the eyes. She liked Carter. She liked him as much as she did any man that was hired to perform the same task as she was. She had no reason to dislike him. Her feelings toward him were more of a competitive nature rather than a hatred. Now that she is looking at him in his current state, she fears that maybe her past has led her to act in an extreme manner which was unwarranted. Has she been too harsh with the men in her life? Is that why she is still single and hasn't had a date since moving to Twisted Timbers two months ago? She knows she shows a hard exterior, but she has been treated unfairly in the past because of her gender, and she refuses to let it happen again.

She gets up from the ground, happy that there was nobody else in the room to witness her fall. She decides she has punished the man enough, but not without gathering a mouthful of saliva and spitting it on the man while she stands over top of him. Her mind drifts to the woman in the other part of the cave. She dusts herself off and draws her weapon again. Slowly she exits the room with the large fire and searches the other rooms for the one that holds the injured woman.

On the third try, she finds the room where the body of the missing hiker is lying in the corner. It is exactly as Mitch described it to her. The body of Erin Winkler appears to be dead, tucked in the corner and surrounded by large leaves, branches and assorted vines. Immediately Sloane thinks that the woman looks a lot like herself. Their bodies and features are very similar. The fact that the person laying helpless on the floor of this cave could have been her, gives her even more reason to reflect on how she's been living her life. Why is she not afraid in situations like this? She knows the answer once again is buried in her past and her determination to succeed in her current line of work, at any cost.

She wonders how old the woman is who is lying on the ground in front of her. She looks at the motionless body as if it is her own, covered in blood and missing a few important body parts. She decides to kneel next to the body and talk to the woman. Her words come out soft and gentle, very unlike how she would normally talk to a stranger. Her tone is lacking the same coarseness that she has adopted since the loss of her father and brother. She has grown accustomed to being on the defensive with almost everyone, trying to exceed expectations even if there are none.

The muscles in her face loosen and her heart begins to melt for the woman. Her life will never be the same, even if she makes it out of here alive. This woman will never be able to talk again, and Sloane Nichols begins to feel guilty for taking the privilege of speaking to others for granted all this time. She places her gun on the ground and reaches for the good hand of the woman, the only hand of the woman. Her skin is cool to the touch, causing Sloane to fear the woman is already dead. Regardless, she takes the hand and rubs it between her own. She hasn't said a real prayer since the funeral for her brother, but now seems like just as good of a time as any.

She utters the words to the prayer in a quiet tone, so only the two women in the cave can hear what is being said. She continues to rub the lady's hand, trying to warm it up and look for any sign of life. She hasn't felt a pulse, but she hasn't really been looking for one either. She finishes the prayer and makes the sign of the cross, first for herself and then moves the arm of the woman for her to do the same. She lays the arm across her chest and inches away from the body. She rolls back on her heels to raise herself off the ground and uses her palms to brush the dirt off her knees and then to wipe away the tears from her face. She then reaches for her gun that she had put on the ground beside the woman's body. It isn't there. Her heart skips a beat. She turns quickly, frantically searching for her police-issued weapon when she is met with a strong blow to the head. She didn't see it coming until it was too late. She lets out a very loud, feminine scream as her body goes flying across the room. Before she blacks out she can see the man coming toward her. This man is much smaller than the other, but just as dingy. She tries to stop him with a kick, but it misses the target. He reaches for her head, grabs a handful of her hair and thrust her skull against the rock wall of the room. His rotting teeth are the last thing she sees before everything goes dark.

# Kevin M. Moehring

# *Chapter 29*

Stuart Johnson is dutifully following behind Sheriff Thompson. Both men have their weapons drawn and are walking down the steep grade that leads away from the cave. Mitch walks with a purpose, as if he knows exactly where they are going. Stuart, on the other hand, is simply following. It would be an overstatement to suggest they are following a path in the traditional sense. The floor growth has been matted down but the path has not been used enough to allow the dirt from the ground to peek through. The sun has reached its peak in the afternoon sky and the humidity that comes along with it is taking a toll on the dehydrated officers.

Stuart finally decides to break the silence, more out of boredom than anything else. "Sheriff, do you have any idea where we are headed or are we just out here hoping to run into the guy?"

The sheriff stops and turns to face the older deputy, "I thought you knew. When I was brought to the cave, I was pulled behind a horse. A horse that is no longer at the opening of the cave. I am following these tracks, hoping they will lead us to where the other guy is."

"Um… OK. I was just making sure you saw them too." Stuart's face has turned red and he regrets having asked such a stupid question. He is following this man because this man is the sheriff. Of course, he knows where they are going, or at least he has a logical explanation why they are heading in this direction. "I just don't think we should get too far away from the cave in case something happens, and we need to get back to help out Deputy Nichols."

Mitch nods, "she's a strong woman in case you haven't noticed. She can take care of herself. We need to find this other guy, the other brother if we go by your theory. That is the only way we can put this ordeal to rest." He turns away from Stuart and begins walking down the side of the hill.

The ground begins to level out and the growth becomes thicker. It has gotten harder for the two men to continue along the same pathway. At times, they move a little to the left and other times the right is the easiest way to go. Neither man pays much attention to the direction they are heading and before long they have circled back to where they had strayed from the path minutes earlier. They give each other a sheepish look, Stuart follows his with a grin. Mitch is less than enthused.

Stuart begins to say something, obviously going to make light of the situation. Mitch holds a single finger to his mouth, telling Deputy Johnson to stay quiet. They can both hear a sound coming from their right, the opposite direction from which they broke away from the path. The foliage is much thicker in that area and makes Mitch bring out his flashlight to see through it, even though it's mid-afternoon. Once again, the two men look at each other, this time Stuart shows the face of a man whose fear has risen to the surface once again.

Mitch makes the first move, using his elbow to clear out space in the thick brush. He backs his way in as best he can, holding certain branches back so they don't swing back and catch Stuart in the face. The two men move slow and as quiet as possible. If they can achieve the element of surprise, it would more than make up for their inexperience when dealing with strangers in the woods. They inch closer to the brighter light on the other side of the trees, obviously a clearing in the brush.

Mitch can see what he has been chasing since they left the cave, or at least the back half of it. He waits for Stuart to join him at the edge of the brush, two men surprising another would be more imposing than if Mitch leapt out by himself. Together the two men raise their weapons, both checking to make sure they had turned the safeties off. In unison, they emerge from the trees out into the clearing. They are disappointed to see that the only thing waiting for them is the horse, who has been tied to a tree. Both men rapidly check the area around the horse, looking for any sign that someone else is there with them. Having found nothing, the men turn their attention to the ground. Stuart is the first to find the footprints.

Mitch bends down next to the set of prints and points out to Stuart that whoever made them is not wearing shoes, just like the man they have tied up in the cave. They begin to follow the tracks, making their way through more vines and shrubs. When the slope begins to rise the two men stop at the same time. They share a look, letting each other know that they have both figured out the same thing at the same time. If the horse was tied to the tree to keep them busy and look in that area for the other man, it is possible that the person they are chasing has doubled back and is at the cave with Deputy Nichols.

Before either one of the two men can utter a sound, they hear a high-pitched scream come from further up the hill. Their eyes quickly move in the direction of the sound, then back at each other. Their feet begin moving at the same time, Mitch taking the lead on his much older deputy. Branches are scraping against his face as he hurries up the side of the hill, hopefully heading in the same direction as he heard the scream. Mitch stumbles over a huge rock, almost doing a complete somersault before landing on his back. He jumps up about the same time that Stuart also trips over the same well-hidden boulder and lets out an expletive or two as his body lands hard onto the forest floor. He helps Stuart to his feet and turns him around to face the opening of the cave. Mitch is confident that this is where the female scream came from and now wishes he would not have been stupid enough to leave Sloane alone in the cave while they were out looking for the other man. He knows he must get in there, in case there is still a chance that she is alive, but he also knows that if he is too late, he will never be able to forgive himself.

## *Chapter 30*

The two men gather at the entrance to the cave, Mitch taking the lead of course, and Stuart following behind. Sheriff Thompson listens intently, knowing that if there were any activity taking place, it would likely be coming from the room at the far end of the cave. Once he is confident that he hears nothing, he whispers for Stuart to stay put as he crosses the front of the opening and takes up a position on the opposite side. The bright afternoon sun has slowly given way to the much warmer colors of the late evening hours, mixing with the slight bit of light that is coming the cave entrance from the fire.

With three fingers held up. Mitch counts down to signify that it's time to head in. The men stay close to the walls of the cave, with weapons drawn. There is enough light from the fire that they don't need their flashlights. They step slowly, being cautious to not make any more noise than is necessary. Stuart swings his weapon to his left, to inspect the first of the rooms that line the walkway. Mitch does the same and stares into the room where he was once held captive. Their movements are quick, and their stares return to the same point in front of them once they are satisfied the small rooms hold no danger.

The dirt path bends slightly to the left just past the next set of smaller rooms. It isn't severe enough that you would notice it if you were walking, but it allows Mitch the chance to inch further and further until he can see directly into the fire room. Stuart is unable to see around the bend without making himself vulnerable to being seen. A shadow passes, darkening the path for a brief, tense second. Mitch takes another small step and can now see the entire fire. He turns to look at his deputy when movement catches his eye once more. He looks back toward the room at the end of the hall and catches site of the second man for the first time.

The hairs on his arm stand at attention as if he had just seen a ghost. He remains still, hoping to maintain his invisibility while still gathering as much intelligence as to what is happening in the room and the whereabouts of Deputy Nichols. He was stupid for leaving her all alone in the cave, he knows that now. He can only hope that they aren't too late, and they are able to rectify the situation. He hears a small grumble, unmistakably the voice of a man. "Cut me loose, Junior."

Before Mitch can fathom the ramifications of the fact that the male voice just called the other one by name, and Stuart was in fact correct in his theory, a dark figure enters the walkway. He moved quickly out of the room and came to an abrupt stop once he saw the two deputies. Stuart remained motionless, while Mitch aimed his weapon at the man and told him to stop. The sheriff walked confidently toward the man, his gun trained on the shaggy figure the whole time. He closely resembles the man that they had in custody but is not as tall but equally as thick. The man has legs that could very easily double as tree trunks. The hair covering his face is much grayer than his brothers, but just as thick and knotted.

After two steps by the sheriff, the man darts back into the room and behind the wall to the left. Mitch pauses for a moment and gives Stuart a look to let him know that they are going in. Stuart rolls his and shakes his head in a single motion. They both give a quick visual inspection of their weapons and rapidly cover the last few feet into the room.

Mitch is the first to enter the room. He does so with a few side steps so that he can face the two men, leaving his back side exposed to anything that would be on the other side of the room. When he left the cave, there was nothing over there that would need his attention. Stuart follows him into the room but with much less graceful movements. Mitch is nearly knocked over by the older deputy who is struggling to match the side steps that the Sheriff took and is pulling off his version of a dance move instead. Stuart regathers his footing and the two men stand side by side, with their weapons drawn. Stuart is showing his nervousness by moving his arms, and weapon, from one man to the other in rapid fashion, apparently unaware of the best place for him to be aiming it.

One man is still bound by the rope as they left him, and the older brother, Junior, is standing near his feet. His figure is intimidating to say the least. Junior moves slightly to the left and reaches down behind him with his right hand. As if pulling a rabbit from a hat and without saying a word, he pulls up the body of Deputy

Nichols by her hair. Her eyes are red, and she has a spot on her forehead that is beginning to turn purple. She's alive, at least for the moment. Seeing their friend in the clutches of the man makes Stuart even more nervous but allows him to point his gun in a specific location, toward the man on the ground. He refuses to aim it at the man who is holding on to Sloane, and in turn, have his weapon pointed in her direction.

Mitch keeps his weapon trained on the older man and gives Nichols a wink. He's not sure what he had hoped to accomplish from winking at her, and he is quite certain that whatever it was, missed its mark. The three men are at a standoff. Sheriff Thompson remains firm and staring at the eyes of the man. He has looked evil in the face once before, but the eyes of this man are much different. His gaze is that of a person who kills out of necessity, rather than from pleasure. A person who feels like they need to kill to survive is far more dangerous than anything the sheriff has ever dealt with before.

Mitch had been focused on the eyes of the man so strongly that he failed to see the man had produced a gun, probably taken from Nichols. The gun looks small in the massive hand, but regardless of how it looks, it is still pointed at the female officer. He has it presses to the side of her head, the muzzle resting on her temple. There are now three guns in this tiny room, all pointing at a different person. Mitch knows that the man across from him has the upper hand, and there are going to be tense moments ahead.

"I got your girl. Give me those guns." The man speaks the words directly to the Sheriff, the hair on his face doesn't move. "Toss them on the ground over to me." His voice is deep and reminds Mitch of how his father would sound early in the morning when he would get Mitch up for school after not getting much sleep.

He knows that they are going to have to give up their weapons eventually, but Mitch is not ready to do so unless he tries to iron out the terms. "We'll give you the guns when you give us Deputy Nichols." Mitch knows that he is playing a deadly game with this man. His brother was not afraid to kill a police officer and it's doubtful that this man has morals that differ.

"Throw them guns over to my brother and I'll throw her over to you. She's no good to us anyhow. Not enough meat on the bones." Again, the man only speaks to the Sheriff. He has obviously sensed the tension that comes from Stuart and knows that the older man is not much of a threat. Mitch hadn't fully understood why the first man was carving up the remains of Deputy Carter, but now that Junior is talking about how much meat Sloane has on her bones, his intentions become clearer.

"I wish that I could trust you, I really do. I think as soon as we throw our guns on the ground, you are going to kill all three of us." Mitch can feel the look he is getting from Stuart and it is burning a hole through his skin. Deputy Johnson fears that Mitch has just given the crazy man with a gun an idea that he may not had previously thought of. "Let's do this. I'll throw my gun over and then you give me Deputy Nichols. Once she is safe, we can talk about my partner giving up his weapon."

Stuart is even more appalled at this notion and his deep sigh lets everyone in the small room know it. Luckily, the brother is not a fan of this idea either. He shakes his head vigorously and pulls the hair of Deputy Nichols tighter. She stares straight at Mitch, scared out of her mind. Her often abrasive personality has faded and the inner softness that she tries so hard to block from view is spilling out. Mitch again gives her a wink and again he regrets it.

"See, I told you I had your girl. I saw that wink. What is she, like your girlfriend?" The man extends his arm and looks at Deputy Nichols from head to toe. He says the words like he is teasing another young boy on the playground at school. Mitch knows that these men have been in the woods for more than half of their life, and their last social interactions from anyone other than each other probably came twenty years ago. These men have no idea how to carry on an adult conversation or think rationally. "I don't care if she is or she isn't. All I know is that I don't trust you cops. You guys always say you're going to do something or be helpful, then you aren't."

Mitch is unsure how many dealings with the police these guys have had over the years, but for some reason they have a hatred for law enforcement. He needs to get into the guys good graces and find a way to do it quickly. He remembers his father telling him often that sometimes you need to do the unexpected. If you can surprise a person, it is much easier to achieve the goal. Mitch decides to do the one thing that the brute of a man would not expect. He bends over and places his gun on the ground near his foot. With a firm kick, the weapon slides across the dirt floor and lands near the waist of Butch, who is still hog tied. Mitch sees the man's eyes follow the gun across the floor until it stops. His evil gaze returns to the sheriff who is standing with his arms crossed. "You don't have to decide what your next move is right away, but I would like to know why you hate cops so bad though." He hopes if he can get the man talking, maybe he can persuade Junior to loosen his stance and free Deputy Nichols.

As if Mitch hit a nerve by the words he said, the man's face turns a bright shade of red. You can see the anger and hatred the man feels written across his face. "Because they let our dad die. They let them all die and did nothing to stop it. They killed our dad!"

Kevin M. Moehring

# *Chapter 31*

Everyone in town has heard the stories about the fire from the people who were around at the time. Mitch heard them all from his father. There was nothing that could be done except to let the fire burn. There was no water supply in the remote area to allow them to subdue the fire, nor was there any kind of rescue attempt that would have been worth trying. It was the media from the larger cities who helped spread the rumors and place the blame on the police force and lack of an adequate fire department. The larger cities have a far greater supply of resources and manpower than Twisted Timbers did at the time.

He remembers vaguely the look on his father's face when the old man would read some of the articles during breakfast. It ate at his soul that people thought he was to blame or he did less than he was capable of. It was several months before the calls stopped coming in to the house, anonymous strangers calling his dad a murderer. Mitch can remember hearing his father crying at night, the first sign that he ever saw of weakness in the man. The elder Thompson sheltered his son from the negativity as best he could and banned the topic from being discussed further in the house. When your father is the sheriff in town, you learn that what he says goes, especially in his own home.

Right here, in this intense situation in the cave, is the first time that Mitch has had to deal with any of the fallout from the fire personally. The man in front of him, who is still holding on tightly to his deputy, feels that the police department is to blame for the death of his father. What little training he has received has in no way given him any insight on how to handle things from here. Hostage negotiation was not at the top of his list of things to learn when he was given the job. He tries to keep his voice calming and the look on his face as one of understanding and empathy.

The indigent man has been rambling on for several minutes about how the police were to blame. How he and his brother could hear the screams coming from inside the blaze. How the cops stood around and did nothing. The gristly voice of the man pauses momentarily, causing Mitch to look up at him and almost begin to speak. Before he has a chance to, the man begins in again. Now he is telling the story of how the two young boys decided to run further into the woods. They ran as far and as fast as they could, until they couldn't hear the screams and smell the odor of smoke and burning flesh.

Mitch finds the whole story a bit fascinating. He listens intently as the man carries on his speech. He talks about finding the cave, how they had to add on to it over the years with countless hours of digging. How they would sneak back over to the cabins to get supplies that they needed from time to time. How they have adjusted to living in the woods and remaining hidden. It's as if the man has been waiting for a very long time to tell his story and now he has the perfect audience. He is also the only person in the room who has moved the slightest muscle since the rant began. His brother is still tied up on the floor, Deputy Nichols still stands stiff as a board at the man's side and Stuart Johnson is holding his gun out on the two men, with hands shaking.

"Junior, I understand what you are saying about the police, and the rest of the story is astounding. You must understand, we had nothing to do with what happened back then. I was just a little boy, Stuart was still in high school and the woman you are holding was somewhere in California."

"Don't tell me what I have to understand. Don't treat us like we are stupid just because we didn't have no schooling." The look of rage in the man returns and Mitch regrets breaking the rhythm of his speech.

"I'm not saying anything about how much education you had. In fact, I am impressed with how you two have managed to survive all of this time." The last sentence he uttered was the most truthful thing he has told the man. The thought of spending countless years in the wilderness is something Mitch can't even begin to fathom. "What we need to do now is figure out what happens from here."

Mitch has this underlying feeling that there is more to the story than what is being told to him. The two boys have lived peacefully in the woods for almost twenty years and have never made a point to be seen or let anyone know that they were out here. Why did they suddenly decide to break their silence and send the package to the police station? They had to know that action would bring about an investigation and send the police out here looking for them. He can only come up with two good reasons why the men would change what had been successful for them all this time. Either they wanted the police to find them, so they could have their revenge, or the life in the woods had become too hard on them and they wanted to be caught. No matter what the boys had in mind, one of the two scenarios is likely going to play out in the next few moments.

The room has become quiet for the last few seconds. Mitch has laid his cards on the table and the other man is weighing out his options. He leaves the gun pressed into the side of Deputy Nichols, refusing to let her go, knowing that she is the one piece of leverage he has in the situation. He turns his attention over to Stuart, who in return tenses up even further than he has been since entering the room. The man gives a menacing scowl at the Deputy, who replies by moving his weapon and aiming it at the man on the ground. The chapped lips of Junior open slightly in a wry smile, revealing the rotting remnants of teeth on the inside of his mouth. He likes being feared and it shows.

"Tell your partner to toss the gun over and I'll give you what you want." He shakes the head of Nichols to let Mitch know what he is referring to, causing Sloane to let out a slight moan. She has remained silent though all of this, standing brave in the arms of a killer.

Mitch looks over at Stuart. He can see that his hand is clinched so tightly onto the handle of the weapon that his knuckles are white. It's as if the older Deputy has tuned out the conversation that has been going on for the last few minutes. He doesn't even bother to look up at the sheriff when the mention of him tossing his gun away comes up. Mitch must verbally call his name to get his attention and instruct him to toss the gun over to the other side of the room.

Stuart is hesitant at first, knowing he is the only person from his side of the fence that is still armed. He doesn't think it's smart to give the bad guys all the guns, even if it means they save the life of Nichols. Mitch speaks up again and tells Stuart in a much firmer tone to toss the gun over to the other side of the cave. Instead of dropping it to the ground near his feet and kicking it across like Mitch did, Stuart uses an underarm motion to toss the gun across. Anyone who knows Stuart would not be surprised that his aim was awful. He missed the target badly and threw the gun much harder than he wanted to, letting it bounce off the back wall and once more off the ground. All parties in the room watched as the gun landed in the center of the large fire pit.

Kevin M. Moehring

## *Chapter 32*

Mitch is initially slow to react. He has been around guns and ammo all his life, so he knows what happens to a loaded gun that has been tossed in the fire. Eventually the shell casing of the loaded round would get hot enough that the bullet would discharge into whatever direction the gun had been pointed. Since it is impossible to know what direction that would be or when the shot would come, it is best to get as far away from the fire as fast as you can.

The slight pause allows more than enough time for Junior Hopkins to toss Nichols to the side and grab his brother and sling him over his shoulder with ease. The two men are out of the cave even before Mitch thinks about moving. The officers help Sloane to her feet and the three deputies begin a slow jog toward the exit moments before the sound of the gun going off. They are relieved to have made it out of the cave unharmed and with Nichols by their side. They are so relieved that at first, they don't see Junior blocking the path that leads down the side of the mountain.

He stands upright, with his still bound brother at his feet and gun pointed at the three members of the Twisted Timbers Police Department. Originally, they had been standing in a line, side by side. Stuart Johnson had other plans and decided to weasel his way to the rear and in doing so, somehow forced Nichols to the front. Now the two men stand behind her, as if she would be able to shelter them from whatever is about to happen. She turns her head and gives both men a look that is eviler than anything they have seen from the man with the gun. Stuart refuses to meet her gaze and Mitch is too focused on the gun pointed at him to respond to her look.

"This has worked out better than I could have hoped. Now I have all three of you in one place. Not even my cross-eyed brother could miss these shots." The man chuckles slightly as he looks at the three, trying to squeeze together as best as they can without getting any closer to the man.

"Make sure you get closer to them before you start shooting. Once the first shot goes off they'll start scattering like rats." These are the first words the man in the rope has said since his brother started the negotiations. Mitch is impressed that the man was smart enough to suggest that his brother should make the shots as easy as possible.

Junior doesn't respond to the words of his brother, but slowly begins walking toward the group. The deputies inch closer and closer to each other. Mitch can feel the shoulder of Stuart pressing against his own. With every step the man takes toward them, Sloane inches back ever so slightly. Mitch can now feel her body pressed against his own. He reaches down to nudge her back and let her know to stop backing up when he feels something hard. He uses his hand to feel around to determine what it is. If the circumstances were different he is certain that this could be considered foreplay.

The man has come so close to the three that they can now smell his musk. They can see into his eyes in a way that was harder to do from a distance. This man is pure evil and the hatred he has for the badge comes from years of animosity. He hates the police and he hates authority in general. Now it is his turn to get the revenge he has been seeking for years. He raises the weapon up high and begins to aim it at the three officers. Mitch does the only thing he can think of to stop the man from pulling the trigger.

"Wait!" The word comes out much louder than he wanted but it has the desired effect. The man lowers the weapon and Mitch continues, "Why now? You have been living out here all these years and have never tried to be seen. Then we get a package delivered on our doorstep that your brother dropped off. I'm just curious to know why you decided you needed to get your revenge now." Mitch doesn't really need to know the answer to the question, although he is curious. It's simply a stall tactic and a last-ditch effort to take the crazed man's mind off killing them.

Junior looks at the Sheriff with a strange look, one that says the vagrant had never considered that. He looks down at the ground for a brief second before responding, "I guess it just got too hard out here. We used to be good at scavenging for food whenever we could. We got a substantial portion of our yearly supply from the amusement park. Since that place has not been opened this year, it has made everything harder up here. We have just about hunted out the area. If you notice, there isn't much wildlife left around here. On top of all of that, people just keep hiking through the woods, our woods. There seems to be more this year than ever before and it's almost impossible to stay hidden. We've been hungry and agitated since the spring. I guess that aggravation turned to wanting to get revenge even more. Then those hikers found our cave and my brother did what he thought he needed to in order to protect our way of life."

"But the park is going to open back up next year. If you can make it through the winter. then you will be able to go back to the lifestyle you had been living." Mitch is trying to keep the man talking for as long as possible.

"Nah, we have no chance of building up enough reserves for the winter. It takes a lot of work to prepare for the long winters. Neither one of us have the energy to start building a reserve now. Even the body of that black cop wouldn't last us but a couple of weeks."

"But we could help you. The town could help you. Once the people in town hear your story, there would be an outpouring of support. Things have changed down there." Just keep him talking Mitch thinks to himself.

The man shakes his head vigorously. "Oh sure. I'm sure the folks down there would love for us to come out of hiding after so many years. We know what they think about the fire. We know they tried to cover up everything that happened, so they could get on with their lives. Now just stop the talking, this is the way it's going to be." The man is talking rapidly, and little drops of spit fly out of his mouth with every word, some getting trapped on the hairs of his beard.

Junior Hopkins raises his gun and points it at the group. He is so close that Mitch can look down the barrel with ease. Junior first points the weapon at Sloane, who uses the instance to once again show her toughness. She stands straight up and stares directly at the man. He smiles and turns the weapon toward Stuart, who is not so brave. The older man has looked death in the face before and didn't like what he saw. Now, he begins to whimper, and tears begin to roll down his face.

Before the man can take any action, Mitch speaks up. "I should be the first one. My father was the Sheriff of the town when the fire happened, and I am the Sheriff now. If you are going to start shooting people, I want to be the first." There is something in the fiber of his being, probably from how his father raised him, that makes him stand forward and be the first to deal with the consequences. Mitch has rarely seen this side of himself, and quite frankly, doesn't care for it much. The man listens to what is said and obliges the sheriff, turning the gun directly to meet Mitch's nose. It is so close to his face that the sheriff can smell the odor of the gun, the oil, steel and gun powder residue has a unique aroma.

The man holds tightly on the handle, his forefinger gripping the trigger. It is apparent from the way he is holding it that he does not have much experience with guns. From this close it is doubtful that the lack of experience will play much of a factor, it's hard to miss at point blank range. Mitch closes his eyes and starts to say a prayer to himself. He is coming with the terms of his death mentally, asking for forgiveness for all his sins. He refuses to open his eyes and give his killer the satisfaction of seeing the fear that would inevitably be seen.

His memories flash through his mind at a rapid pace. He lands on one of himself coming off the football field in high school. He had just sealed the game with an interception and his father hugged him in pride. This may have been the most emotion his father ever showed him when he was growing up. His flashback is abruptly interrupted by a sound, not a gunshot, a more subtle and soothing sound. It's a female voice, it's Sloane's voice. She has stayed quiet for so long, she must have something important to say.

"Hey, Captain Caveman! That's my weapon you're holding. It's a good weapon, a safe weapon."

# *Chapter 33*

**A** safe weapon? What is she trying to say with that statement? She stressed the word safe so prominently that it caused Mitch to think there was a hidden meaning behind the word. It takes Mitch a moment to put the facts together, but once he does he is again amazed at the strength of the woman. How she could think like that in a moment like this is beyond him. She is obviously trying to tell him that the man has not taken the safety off the pistol. This means that nothing will happen when he tries to pull the trigger. Eventually he will figure out what is going on and will have the gun operational, but the safety might give Mitch the time he needs to save their lives.

He opens his eyes and is met with the barrel of the gun. Looking past it is hard but he manages to meet the eyes of Junior. The blank stare coming from the man lets the sheriff know that he needs to act quickly. He begins fumbling around on the backside of Nichols.

Once again, if this were a date, he would consider this getting to second base. He can slide his hand under her loose-fitting shirt and wrap his hand around the metal object he felt earlier. He uses his other hand to extend the waistband of her yoga pants to allow the object to slide out freely.

Sheriff Thompson feels slightly more confident now that he is holding a weapon. It doesn't have the power or lethality of a gun, but if used properly, the Taser could have enough of an impact to get them out of this predicament alive. He grips it strongly with his right hand, trying to remember back to the brief training they had on the weapon. He can't recall if it has a safety or not, but he has no other choice but to take his chances.

There is a trust level that officers share with each other. Right now, Mitch is trusting that the decoded message Sloane gave him meant that the gun still has the safety on, which would allow Mitch to fire the Taser and not fear for the man shooting at them while he was being shocked. This bit of information is crucial to the execution of the plan. If Mitch hits the man with the Taser and he is still able to fire off shots, there is still a high probability that those shots will hit one of the three officers. It is a chance he must take. He swings his right arm out from behind Nichols and puts the weapon in front of both of their faces. Before the man can react, Mitch pulls the trigger and can see the electrodes exit the weapon and hit their intended target. One of the small metal hooks embeds itself into the left cheek of Junior while the other becomes lodged in the middle of his neck.

The man's body tenses up instantly. He hits the floor and low groans escape his mouth. The surge of electricity causes the man to thrash about more than Mitch had expected. Deputy Nichols is the first one to react and swiftly kicks the gun from the man's hand. Mitch follows by placing a knee in the back of the fallen brother. He reaches for his thick arms but needs help from Nichols to get them behind his back. Stuart is slow to react, clueless to the fact that anything was about to go down. When Mitch is finally able to secure the man's arms, he looks up in time to watch Deputy Johnson fly through the air and land with his body on top of Butch Hopkins, in classic wrestling fashion.

Mitch calls out that he needs a set of handcuffs and Stuart is quick to provide them. The sheriff was unaware they were missing from his tool belt until this very moment. He rolls over the new prisoner and removes the probes from his cheek and neck. The man doesn't make a sound. The craziness has now left his face and he looks defeated. The officers stand over the two men, Stuart giving the others energetic hugs. He is happy to still be breathing, as are the other two. They take a moment to gather themselves, each looking to make sure the others are alright. Mitch walks to Deputy Nichols and inspects her head. She has a nasty welt and some dried blood under her nose, but other than that she seems to be fine.

"We need to get these guys up and start heading out of here. Stuart, go back in that other room and get some more rope so we can tie the two of them together. Sloane, can you go around the cave and gather up our guns and other belongings. I'm going to undo the ropes around Butch's feet, so he can walk out of here on his own. I'm sure the Feds will be coming up the side of the hill at any time." At least Mitch hopes they will be.

The officers scatter and hurry about the tasks given to them. None of them care to stay up in these woods any longer than they must. Night has fallen again and the trek out of this location is only going to get more treacherous the longer they wait. Now that he is away from the other two, Mitch can finally breathe a sigh of relief. He had no idea how they were going to get out of the situation, but somehow, they managed. He makes a mental note to commend Deputy Nichols on her quick thinking. If she hadn't pointed out the fact that Junior had failed to turn off the safety on her weapon, there is a high likelihood that they would all be dead.

Stuart and Sloane return to the mouth of the cave at the same time. She gives the two men their weapons right away and Stuart begins the task of tying the two prisoners together. He loops the first end of the rope around the handcuffs that are holding Junior and does a similar loop around the rope holding the hands of Butch. It will be too difficult for the two men to try and make a run for it through the tough terrain if they are tied together. Mitch inspects the knots that were made to make sure they were tight and directs the two brothers to start walking. He is not afraid to use their knowledge of these woods to his advantage by having them lead the group out of here on the easiest route.

Their progress is stopped almost immediately when Sloane asks the sheriff if they are just going to leave the injured woman in the cave. He had almost forgotten about Erin Winkler, but he knows there isn't much they can do for her. He explains to the female deputy that if they try to move her out of these woods on their own, it will probably just cause more damage. There is no sense in any of them staying behind and staying with her, as there isn't much they can do for her and the manpower is better served in getting these two brothers out of the forest.

Deputy Nichols reluctantly agrees and starts walking along one side of the men, closest to Butch. Stuart Johnson marches on the opposite side, nearest Junior. Sheriff Thompson is a few paces behind them and right in the middle of the two barefooted men. He looks at them with a slight bit of envy. Two boys managed to survive in these woods for almost two decades without any form of help from the outside world. They were able to feed themselves, provide shelter and water, and very well could have lived the same lifestyle for many more years had their food supply not run dry. It is truly too astonishing for Mitch to comprehend.

The group is making decent time as they reach the cabins which once housed the men from the mill. Nichols and Johnson keep their flashlights pointed in front of the two men to show them where obstacles are. Everyone is silent. Mitch imagines that the prisoners are somewhat relieved that their life in the woods has come to an end. The other two deputies are probably feeling much like he is, thankful to be alive. They make their way past the cabins and across the large opening where the mill once stood. Still the group remains silent. When they reach the trees once again, they are met with flashlights numbering in the dozens. Mitch calls out to identify himself and is met with an equally welcoming reply. The F.B.I. has finally shown up to the crime scene.

Mitch could say a lot of derogatory things about the Bureau, but at this point, he is very happy to see them. When they show up to a crime scene, they come out in full force. There are numerous agents scattered throughout the trees, each one with their weapon drawn. Agent Walker makes his way to the front of the group and shakes the hand of the Sheriff. They make small talk for a bit and Mitch gives him the rundown on the events that transpired. He tells Walker about their deputy who has been chopped to pieces and left in the cave, along with the barely breathing body of the missing hiker.

"Looks like you guys have this all wrapped up. My guys will take the prisoners and we'll get statements from the three of you in the morning." Agent Walker has treated Mitch with the utmost respect on both meetings, the same cannot be said for the other agents the Sheriff has had to deal with. Mitch nods at the agent and the three officers continue their march out of the woods. Stuart once again slides down the hill that leads to Hidden Creek, this time he is unable to keep his balance and he slides down on his butt, cursing the entire way and ruining the uniform slacks he worked diligently to protect.

Their cars are parked in the same gravel parking lot near the trail head, but since Mitch has been unable to locate the keys to his vehicle, the three head toward Johnson's sedan. When Johnson and Nichols returned to the woods in the morning there were only two cars in this lot, now there are lights and sirens filling the night sky. They are all relieved to see that the federal agents have already moved the body of Robert Eldridge, who had been hanging over the creek, and have it loaded in a coroner vehicle in the same lot. They see several agents keeping busy, none of them even bothering to look up long enough to make eye contact with the trio.

Mitch can feel the muscles in his thighs burning from the strenuous hike and the lack of water. He is too competitive to complain or let on to the others that he is in pain. He looks at his team and is proud of the way they were able to pull together and survive the ordeal. He wonders how much longer Stuart Johnson is going to remain a police officer or has the last few months pushed him over his limits.

He studies Sloane Nichols, who walks briskly a few feet in front of him as they head for Stuart's car. He wonders where things with her will go from here. He noticed a slight change in her after leaving her in the cave alone, but he's not sure what it is. Will the feeling he gets in the pit of his stomach every time he sees her ever go away?

Stuart reaches the car first and heads straight for the trunk and begins passing out bottles of water. The three all smile and begin drinking right away. Mitch looks back at the woods long enough to ponder what else may be happening in the forest that he has no idea about.

Even after everything that has taken place in these woods the last couple of days, the moonlight finds a way to make the whole area look peaceful and calm. The three turn and notice the Hopkins brothers have been led out of the woods and are being ushered into the back of one of the dark sedans. An agent in a dark blue jacket slams the door shut and the three officers celebrate a job well done with another drink of water.

# *Chapter 34*

The ride back to town is a quiet one. Mitch sits in the passenger seat of the car and stares blankly out the window. Nichols is seated in the back and has not said a word for the entire trip. Stuart, who is driving, has fiddled with the radio enough times to cause Mitch to reach over and turn it off, but has not said a word either. They occasionally spot another federal vehicle heading up to the crime scene, but the road is otherwise quiet. It's almost nine on a Saturday night and most of the tourists are either in for the night or have taken their seats at one of the bars in town.

Mitch smiles when he sees the ambulance pass them heading in the opposite direction. This means the girl in the cave is still alive. Unfortunately, the ambulance is followed closely by another coroner's van, a haunting reminder that he lost an officer today. Out of nowhere, Mitch decides now is as good of a time as any to get to know the female officer in the back seat a little better.

"Sloane, when you came to town and joined the department, we were kind of in a bind and had to throw you to the wolves right away." He tries to ease into the question with as much tact as he can muster. "I'm afraid I don't know much about you. We have a few minutes until we get back to town, why don't you tell us what we need to know."

Sloane is caught off-guard at first, but slides her phone shut and sits up in the seat. Her face peeks through to the front seat, between the two male officers. "Well, I was born and raised in Southern California by my father, my mom died when I was very young. My dad was on the L.A.P.D, as was my brother. Both were killed in the line of duty, one during a robbery gone wrong and the other by some gang banger." Her tone is steady, no sign of emotion or pain. "I decided I wanted to follow in their footsteps and joined the academy. I excelled in every test, both mental and physical. Two days before graduation, I was told that the people at the top of the totem pole had decided I was not L.A.P.D. material. They gave me some lame excuse, but I know it was because I was a female, not to mention they didn't want me to be the third member of my family to die in their employment." She pauses briefly, only long enough to take along drink from her water bottle. "About the same time, I saw the stories about what happened up here, the thing at the amusement park. I figured you'd be needing some bodies to make it through the summer, and here I am."

Stuart and Mitch steal a glance at each other. Their mind is blown that she is opening up to them like this. Mitch was not expecting this much information to come out of her mouth. He turns back to look at the woman just as she puts the cap back on her bottle and adjusts herself in the seat before beginning again. "I worked my tail off to get into shape and learn everything I would need to be a good cop. I wanted to be like my dad and my brother. I ran faster, shot straighter and drove better than any of the men there. I was so close to getting what I wanted and then I had it all stripped away. From that day on I have had this feeling inside that causes me to compete more fiercely with the people around me, especially the men."

She has been spouting the words for the last several minutes, rarely stopping long enough to take a breath. They have reached the center of town by the time she has finished, and Mitch just gives her a nod. Neither man knows how to respond to her, but they hope it is one of those things that doesn't require a response at all. Maybe it is just something she needed to get off her chest and they were the ones chosen to listen. Mitch motions to Stuart to pull into Maddie's Diner. It has been almost two days since the Sheriff had anything to eat and his stomach is growling.

The parking lot to the diner is nearly empty, being well past the dinner rush, so Stuart has no problem getting a parking spot near the front door. Nichols jumps out of the back of the car and rushes inside to use the restroom, obviously unfazed by the topic of conversation for the last few minutes. The two men exit the car and look over the top of the vehicle at each other. "Sheriff, do you have any idea what that was all about?"

"I haven't the foggiest. Maybe something hit her up in that cave alone and she had a come to Jesus moment. Who knows?" Mitch knows there is probably more to the story than what they were given, but now is not the time to prod the woman further for details. "You go inside and get us a table, looks like I have a fan coming out here to meet me."

Stuart turns and peers through the glass window and sees the mayor of Twisted Timbers heading for the exit, practically in a sprint. Deputy Johnson nods and heads into the diner. Mitch knew that he would have to answer to the mayor, but he was hoping to task would hold off until the morning. It has not.

Mayor Billings slides past Stuart and spills out of the building and meets Mitch with an angry stare. His face is red and flush, which it seems to be every time he has a meeting with Mitch. The portly man stands in front of the sheriff and straightens the jacket of his finest J.C. Penny suit. "Would you like to explain what the hell has been going on?"

Mitch returns his look with a disgusted face of his own. If the mayor knew what the sheriff had been through in the last couple of days, he might not be so ill-mannered. "You'll get the report in the morning, I'm sure you've seen the feds driving around."

"Darn right I did and not a single police officer to be found for the entire day. One of the busiest days of the year and our police department is being ran by a sixty-year-old woman." Mitch had not considered the ramifications of leaving the town without an active officer, nor the fact that poor Lucille Pennington was left to deal with the station all by herself.

"Looks like the town is still standing." Mitch is only half joking when he says this to Mayor Billings and throws his right arm to show the mayor that the town is indeed still intact. "Like I said, you'll see the full report in the morning. Now if you'll excuse me, I have not eaten in a while and would like to do so."

Mitch watches the chubby man with the greased back hair storm off. He had expected that to take much longer but maybe the mayor was able to read the exhaustion in Mitch's eyes and gave him the benefit of the doubt, which would be a first for anyone dealing with Mayor Billings. Just when Mitch begins to head into the diner, he sees the man stop short of getting in his car and head back to where the sheriff is standing. "There are big plans in the work for this town. I am making things happen. We have representatives from the Reynolds

Corporation coming to town this week with plans to build a new resort. I need to have your word that you are up to the task of keeping the people who come here safe."

"As always Mayor, it's been a pleasure talking to you." Mitch has been raised to always show respect to the people he deals with. Tonight, his manners have taken a backseat to the wants and needs of his body. He gives the mayor a slight smile and turns his back on the man.

When he enters the restaurant, he finds Nichols sitting at a table alone and assumes that Stuart took the opportunity to go to the restroom himself. He quickly pulls a menu out and starts reading over the dinner choices, hoping this will provide enough resistance to stop any conversation from starting until Stuart returns. Unfortunately, it does not.

"I know I sounded like a crazy person in the car, giving you guys my whole life history. I just saw that girl in the cave and thought it could have very easily been me. It made me think about how I was living my life and pushing away anyone that got close to me." She says this while twirling around her straw inside the glass of water sitting in front of her, refusing to make eye contact with Mitch.

"We experienced some strange things up there. It affects everyone differently. Look at Stuart, normally he is cool and calm, but you get him out in the field where there could be some real danger and suddenly he's the second coming of Benny Hill or the Three Stooges." He smiles at her just as Stuart joins them and sits down in the chair next to Mitch.

The three order their meals and eat in almost silence. No one is willing to begin the discussion about the events that took place in the woods, knowing that they will have to repeat their stories several times for the F.B.I. in the coming days. It's nice to sit and enjoy a meal without having to worry about the consequences of what just happened to them. Mitch wonders how the group must look to the staff of the diner, Stuart covered in mud, Sloane with her bruised face and Mitch disheveled from top to bottom. He laughs to himself and digs into his food.

Stuart finishes his meal first and asks Mitch about his conversation with the mayor. "As you could imagine he was not happy. He kept saying there is some rich woman who is supposed to come to town and build a big resort style hotel and the mayor is afraid if we keep having things like this happen, it would scare her and her money away."

Sloane perks up at the sound of a rich woman coming to town. There have been several times that Mitch has seen her at the station with a stack of magazines, all of which keep their readers current on the newest celebrity gossip. "A resort hotel huh? Did the mayor give you a name of the lady?"

Mitch was not expecting to be asked that question and pauses briefly while he tries to pull the name from his memory. "It's Reynolds I think. The Reynolds Corporation is what he said I believe."

"Doesn't sound familiar, oh well." Nichols finishes the last of her fries and tosses her used napkin onto her empty plate. She looks over at Stuart and smiles at him. "Stuart, you know what? I just realized something. We have something very special in common. We have both saved the precious life of our dear Sheriff."

Stuart practically spits out his drink at the sound of these words. Mitch turns red in the face before grabbing the check and throwing cash on the table. "Yes, you two are in an elite class and to thank you, I will pay for dinner. Now go home and get some rest. We are all in for a long day tomorrow."

# *Chapter 35*

The sun breaks through the window in his bedroom and as reluctant as he is, Mitch manages to make his way out of bed and get a much-needed shower. As the steam fades from the room and he gets the first view of himself in the mirror, he sees that his body is showing the signs of the beating it took. The dark discoloration on his abdomen look worse than it feels, but his ribs are tender to the touch. He looks at his face where several scratches are scattered about.

He runs the towel through his damp brown hair and as usual, he lets his brown locks fall where they may. He has never cared much about his appearance, and today he does not have enough energy to change his ways. He throws on a clean uniform and looks on the table next to the bed for his phone. He places a call to

Lucille Pennington. He takes several minutes to explain to the woman the events in the woods and asks her to pick him up on the way to the station, which she is happy to do.

Lucille arrives in front of his apartment rather quickly and announces herself with a honk of her horn. He locks the door behind him and climbs into the passenger seat of the minivan, greets the woman and instructs her to head out toward Hidden Creek. Mitch could have gotten a ride to the crime scene from any one of the numerous federal agents that would be heading that way, but right now he wants to be nearer the people he knows, and Lucille makes him feel at ease. She reminds him of a grandmother, always positive and encouraging.

He goes more into detail about what went on in the woods and the death of Deputy Carter. Lucille gives the standard reply that she didn't really care for him, but she would never wish him to be dead. She also informs Mitch that in the forty-five years she has worked at the station, there had never been an officer killed, until a few months ago. Mitch is doing his best to carry on a conversation with the woman, even though the last thing he wants to do right now is relive the events.

Mitch is happy when Lucille finally pulls the van into the parking lot, that is now filled with dark sedans. He climbs out and thanks her for the ride, reminding her that the other two officers will be at the station as will the agents from the F.B.I. He waves to her as he walks away and tries to avoid the agents as he makes his way into the woods.

He struggles to make his way down the steep and hill and across the creek. His footing isn't as firm as would be if his muscles were fresh. Even though he is having a rough time, Mitch manages to make it to the ridge on the opposite side of the creek much easier than some of the agents who are not used to dealing with this kind of environment. He passes several of them who are heading the other direction carrying large black plastic bags. Mitch at first assumes that they are carrying out bags of evidence, knowing that the Bureau is a huge fan of gathering as much information as possible and sorting out the details later. It takes a few minutes before Mitch realizes the contents of the bags is more than just evidence, it's the severed remains of Officer Carter.

At first, Mitch is upset that they have decided to carry out his body in nothing more than garbage bags. After walking on further and allowing his anger to subside, he realizes that there are not many other options to carry out pieces of a human body other than garbage bags. He continues his hike into the woods and before long comes to the area where the saw mill once stood. He takes a few seconds to look over the stash of dead flowers that Nichols found, but now hold a new meaning. He now knows that they were left here by two boys who lost everything they had during the fire, and heard the screams of the men who died, including their father.

He stops at the cabins long enough to peer inside each of them, noticing what few items that were once on the inside were already removed as evidence. His walk becomes slower, and fewer agents pass by as he makes his way to the mouth of the cave. He only sees three agents on the inside of the cave, one guarding the entrance, one on the inside taking pictures and a third who has been given the task of keeping an eye on the remaining parts of Carter which have not been bagged up.

He has no trouble getting past the agent at the entrance, obviously the man has been given instructions to allow Sheriff Thompson to go where he pleases. Much like how the fear evaporates when you finally find the light switch in a dark basement, the cave does not have nearly the same ominous feeling as it did yesterday. It is much better lit, and the lack of danger allows Mitch to look through the remaining rooms at his leisure. He came to the cave with one thing in mind, to get back into the room with the newspaper articles that had been hanging on the walls.

He is relieved that most of the news clippings are still hanging on the walls like they were the day before. The headlines have not changed overnight, but Mitch reads the articles over in more detail anyway. He spends several minutes studying the articles, reading every word on some and barely perusing others. His concentration is broken when an agent enters the small room where he is standing.

"Sheriff Thompson, I was told to give you these if I saw you." The agent extends his hands and gives Mitch his keys and set of cuffs. Mitch takes them and sticks the keys in his pocket and the cuffs in his waistband. Without saying a word, the sheriff leaves the room and walks out of the cave, beginning the long walk out of the woods.

His truck is parked further down the creek, where he parked it on Friday morning when he first made the trip out here with Deputy Nichols. There is no one else in this part of the forest, allowing Mitch the silence that he craves. He feels like he has gotten more information regarding the fires from the walls of the cave than he got at any point in his life, including from his father. He understands how the boys can blame the police for the fate of their father and the other men, but that doesn't give them the right to do the things they have.

He is not thinking about how badly his thighs are burning or the blisters on his feet as he crosses the creek and begins the climb back up to the road. These woods have always held a special piece of Mitch's heart, his happy place. He vows to not let these two men take that away from him. He clears the guardrail in a single step and unlocks the door to his truck. Once inside he starts the engine and breaks down in tears, tears he has been fighting back for two days.

## *Chapter 36*

He sits in the truck, allowing it to idle and allowing himself to release the emotions that he normally holds inside. He is dreading the coming hours and the interrogations that are sure to come, so he is in no hurry to head back to the station. His phone vibrates in his pocket, but he doesn't even reach for it. He turns the volume on the radio up high and puts the truck into gear and begins the trip.

He drives slowly, trying to waste as much time as he can. He keeps his head down as he passes the parking lot where the agents are all gathered. He taps his hand along to the beat of the song playing on the radio, a song he doesn't know the words to. The winding road that he has traveled many times in his life goes by quickly, much quicker than he would like it to. As he pulls into town, he hopes the lone red light will slow his pace, which it does not.

Every spot in the small parking lot outside of the police station is full, except for the one marked for the sheriff. He pulls into the spot and exits the truck. He is normally eager to get into the office, but this morning is different. Not only did he not stop and have his normal breakfast, which his stomach is starting to remind of, but he is walking into a storm of agents who are going to start hounding him for answers from the minute he walks in.

He marches up the steps and holds the glass door for two agents who are coming out just as he is going in. They look at him, only long enough to nod and brush past him. The inner office space of the station has once again been taken over by the dozens of agents from Portland. Men and women scurry about in the confined spaces, and papers are being shuffled at rapid speed. He looks to his left and smiles at a familiar face. Sloane Nichols is seated at her desk and is being questioned by an agent who is scribbling fast in his notebook. She matches his look and returns a smile; which Mitch takes to mean that she is holding up. Knowing what he does about the woman now, Mitch expected nothing less.

Stuart is also seated at his desk, but he is alone. Mitch slides over to him and sees that the man took time this morning to properly shave and has the normal clean-cut look that Mitch is used to seeing. Before he can say anything to Deputy Johnson, Mitch hears the voice of Agent Walker above the crowd. He calls Mitch into the Sheriff's office and asks him to have a seat. Mitch feels odd sitting on the opposite side of his own desk, but he obliges to get this part of the day over as quickly as possible.

"Looks like you guys had an exciting weekend up here," Walker begins.

"I guess you can say that." Mitch would use several words to describe the weekend, such as exhausting or frightening, but exciting wouldn't have been his first choice.

Agent Walker sits down at the desk, Mitch's desk, surrounded by stacks of papers and files. The sheriff has no idea what could possibly be on all the paperwork, none of it was there the last time he was seated at his own desk. Walker begins reading from one of the papers, running down the events of the last couple of days. Mitch nods in agreeance at everything that is being read back to him. There isn't much more that he can add to the story that the feds have not already gotten from the other two officers. Agent Walker nods and puts the piece of paper back on top of the pile.

"Sheriff, we're not going to stay here in your way for much longer. You know how this goes, we need to cover all of the bases." He looks at Mitch with more respect than he did last time the two met. Mitch knows this is because the small-town cops were able to handle the case themselves, only needing the federal officers to hold the prisoners and go forward with the charges.

"Unfortunately, I do. I still need to write up my formal report. Mayor Billings is breathing down my neck." Mitch hadn't forgotten the ultimatum he was given by the mayor, but he was not looking forward to the paperwork that is required to fulfill the task. He never likes the paperwork.

Agent Walker rises from the chair and exits the room without saying another word. Mitch takes the opportunity to regain control of his desk and begin writing down his version of the events. He is thorough, making note of everything he can think of that could have an impact on the case for both the attorneys who will try the case, and the mayor who is just nosey.

Several times through the next few hours, Walker would reenter the room and fill Mitch in on new developments. The woman from the cave, Erin Winkler, succumb to her injuries and passed away around lunch time. It was inevitable in the eyes of the sheriff, but judging by the reaction of Deputy Nichols, she had thought the woman was going to be alright.

Mitch watches as she is told the information from a different agent, gets out of her chair and storms off to the locker room, visibly shaken. Maybe she did change when she was alone in the cave. The Sloane he has seen so far would never let her emotions get the best of her.

Just as Sheriff Thompson is finishing up with his reports, Agent Walker comes into his office and takes a seat. The man has a look on his face that tells Mitch that he is not going to like what the agent has to say. "We are just about done with the things we can do here. Honestly, there wasn't much evidence to collect. I need to prepare you for a few things that may come up in the next couple of days or weeks."

The serious nature of the man's tone gives Mitch cause for concern. "Walker, you know what happened up there. I'm not sure anything you can tell me now would catch me off-guard."

"I know you have been through a lot in the last few months. More shit than most men deal with in a lifetime. I just want you to know that I have every intention of making sure these guys are prosecuted to the fullest extent of the law." He crosses his legs and waits for a response from Mitch.

"I'm not sure what you are trying to tell me. These guys are killers. They've killed at least three people, including a police officer. Are you trying to tell me that they may get off?"

"That's not what I'm saying at all. I can give you the facts as we have them now, but it is very early. Most of the evidence we collected was no good. It's hard to preserve a body and collect trace when it is being dangled over a creek in the woods. There were no fingerprints to find in the cave considering the whole place was nothing but dirt. Our best chance at a witness and a person who could testify against the men passed away a few hours ago." He uncrosses his legs and leans in closer to make sure what he is saying is registering in the eyes of the Sheriff. "On top of all of that, the press got hold of the story late last night and since then, every top lawyer in the country is fighting for a chance to represent the two men. It's going to be a lengthy process trying to prosecute them."

"What? Why would any lawyer want to help these two maniacs? They killed one of my guys and butchered his body, not to mention what they did to the two hikers." Mitch had assumed that it was an open and shut case, unaware of how things work in the rest of the country. He has heard stories of murderers being set free on technicalities before, but he didn't think he would ever have to deal with an outcome of that nature.

"I'm not saying they are going to go free, but I can tell you the outpouring of support that these two men will get from the public will be immense." The agent runs his fingers through his black and slightly gray hair, ending with his fingers rubbing his eyes. "I don't like it any more than you do, but like I said, most of the evidence we have is either tainted or hearsay. A good lawyer, and they are bound to get the best simply for the media attention the case will get, will go with an insanity plea. If ever there was a case where insanity is a viable defense, this may be it."

"Walker, you have to do something. They killed Deputy Carter. They killed him and then cut up his body. It's just not right." Mitch is visibly shaken. His trust in the justice system fading with every word out of the mouth of the federal agent.

"I know they killed him and you know they killed him, but the facts are he fell into a bear trap. What they did to the body afterwards was awful, but it was not murder. We will charge them with mutilation of a corpse, but their lawyers will argue that they found the body and were preparing it to store for the winter. I know it sounds hideous but that is how these boys survived up there all this time."

A prolonged period of silence follows, and Mitch is left without much to say. This day is not turning out how he expected it to. He looks past the agent and out into the open offices in front of him. Stuart is once again alone, as is Deputy Nichols. He knows they have not been given the same information that he has. Some details of the case of relayed to the Sheriff, who is then given the job of breaking the news to his deputies, another part of the job he hates.

Walker leaves the room by saying that his agents should be out of his hair in an hour or so. He reiterates that he is going to try to get the prosecutor to go for murder charges and see this thing through. Mitch doesn't respond. The agent leaves the room and Mitch is left at his desk in silence, and disgust.

Kevin M. Moehring

## *Chapter 37*

True to what he was told by Agent Walker, the rest of the F.B.I. investigators leave the police station shortly after their conversation. Mitch pays close attention to his deputies and their reactions and facial expressions. Nichols stands by Stuart and carries on a lengthy conversation before both get up and head toward Mitch's office. He knew they would be heading his way, but he was hoping he had more time to prepare for what he had to tell them.

They knock on his door before entering, even though he can clearly see them through the glass windows. They enter, and Sloane takes the seat opposite the Sheriff, Stuart stands behind her. They sit there in silence staring at Mitch, waiting for him to spill the beans. He begins slowly and lets them know that Erin

Winkler didn't make it. They both were aware of her condition and now they show little to no reaction to the news.

He proceeds to tell them the information he was given by Agent Walker, almost word for word. He hates the words as they stream out of his mouth as if they're his own. They are not. If it were up to him the two men would be thrown in jail for the rest of their lives. Unfortunately, he has no say in the matter. The fate of the two men is left in the hands of people Mitch has never met.

After hearing that the case may not go as smoothly as they had believed, the two deputies are angered. Sloane gets out of the chair and paces around the room. She stops several times and Mitch fears she is going to put her hand through the plate glass window. She holds back her anger well enough to save the glass, but the carpet below her feet is taking the brunt of her emotions. Stuart seems confused by what Mitch has told him.

"Sheriff, I'm just a small-town cop with not much education on what goes on out in the big cities. Are you telling me that these two men, who killed three people including Deputy Carter, are going to go free?" Stuart is obviously embarrassed to ask the question, but he needs to know the answer anyway.

"That's not what I'm saying. Agent Walker was adamant that they were going to pursue murder charges on the two, but he wanted us to be ready for anything, in case the prosecutor decides to go another route."

"Stuart, he's saying that the Hannibal Lecter brothers are going to plead insanity and probably get sent to a mental hospital for a few years. Right, Sheriff." Mitch can see that Sloane Nichols has back her mental edge, the one that keeps her defenses on high alert.

"That's right. Walker said that high powered attorneys are fighting for the chance to defend these guys because of the media attention the case will get. He also said that we should prepare ourselves in case the outcome of the case isn't what we think it should be." Mitch leans back in his chair and folds his hands across his stomach, waiting for the next round of questioning from the officers.

Stuart stands up from his chair and begins to leave the office. He stops and turns back to the Sheriff, "it's not our job to see that the prisoners we capture are put in jail for a long time. Our job consists of keeping the residents of Twisted Timbers safe, no matter the cost. I feel like we did our job exceptionally well this weekend. I will be able to sleep easy knowing this." Sometimes Stuart surprises everyone with the amount of levity that leaves his mouth.

"Stuart, before you go, Agent Walker is assigning two agents to look after the town for the next couple of days. He thinks we need time to rest up and get our minds straight. Make sure you take advantage of this." Mitch makes sure to look at Deputy Nichols as well, so he knows that she also got the message that she can take the next few days off.

"Then I am heading home and going to crawl under my blankets for a few days. My body can definitely use it." He waves at Nichols as he leaves the room. Mitch watches him walk away, with his slight limp, and speak briefly to Lucille before walking out of the police station. Despite all his short comings, Stuart Johnson is a good man and a fine police officer.

Mitch looks at Sloane Nichols, now seated across from him once again. She is probably not taking the news about the future of the case as good as Stuart did. She hasn't said much in the last few minutes and Mitch is not very good at reading women. He is waiting for her to unload on him in a verbal assault that Mitch will not have the energy to fight.

Instead, the blue in her eyes softly look at his face, and she licks her top lip slowly before speaking. "Well Sheriff, looks like it's just the two of us now."

Well that's not at all what Mitch had expected to come out of her mouth. "Yes, it appears it is. Make sure you also take full advantage of the next few days off. The last month of the tourist season is always busy." He tries to keep the focus of the conversation on work, knowing that Sloane has already punched the mental time clock.

"The way I see it, you owe me," she says with a smile.

"I owe you? What do I owe you?" Mitch is confused by her statement, trying to recall if he didn't give her money for the lunch she brought in earlier in the day.

"I saved your life in those woods, and now you owe me." Once again, she looks at him with a smile. Mitch had never noticed the stark contrast between her bleach white smile and her deep blue eyes until this very moment.

"Oh that. I had almost forgot. Well how do you suggest I repay you?" Mitch is starting to understand the playful tone of the conversation and reluctantly partakes.

"Well, I'm thinking I'll let you buy me a drink at the Bottom Dollar." She rises from the chair she had been sitting on and sits on the edge of the desk now.

"A drink? That's all you think my life is worth?" Mitch looks back at her with a smile of his own.

"No Mitch, the drink is just the beginning. I have a long list of ways in which you are going to repay me tonight."

I hope you enjoyed my latest story. Feel free to check out my other books and as always, please remember that reviews are the best way you can support an Indie author.

For the latest news from Kevin M. Moehring including upcoming releases, please follow him on Facebook. https://facebook.com/kevinmmoehring

**<u>Additional books by Kevin M. Moehring</u>**

**Sacrifice**

**Graham Park—Twisted Timbers book 1**

**Evil in the Woods—Twisted Timbers book 2**

**Twisted Timbers book 3 … coming soon**

Made in the USA
Columbia, SC
10 September 2021

45047031R00171